THE
WORLD'S
ONE HUNDRED
BEST SHORT STORIES

VOLUME FOUR
L O V E

THE
WORLD'S
ONE HUNDRED
BEST SHORT STORIES

[IN TEN VOLUMES]

GRANT OVERTON
EDITOR - IN - CHIEF

VOLUME FOUR
L O V E

FUNK & WAGNALLS COMPANY
NEW YORK AND LONDON

CONTENTS

THE WORLD'S 100 BEST SHORT STORIES

YOUTH TO YOUTH

By Konrad Bercovici

Hey, ho! I want to sing to you of the wisdom of the north wind—the gray-blue vulture of the winds who comes from nowhere to throw the flames of the camp-fires skyward and the smoke from the chimneys to the earth.

Hey, ho! Listen to the song of the wisdom of woman; woman wiser and older than wisdom itself.

Hey, ho! Whether they be our mothers or sisters, or daughters or sweethearts, they are a thousand years old when they are born and ten times that when we begin only to see them.

Hey, ho! We believe not what we know. They don't want to know what they believe. They are the north wind. They come from nowhere. They blow out our fires with their laughter and whispers and then fan the cold smoke into our eyes. When we die for what we believe, they laugh. What we call good is good only for us. And they know not what is wrong. When we lie, we tell the truth. When they tell the truth, they lie.

Hey, ho! The north wind rustles the fallen leaves

7

on the ground and bends the stoutest oaks. Woman is wind fashioned by the God Dhundra into flesh and bone. She is as strong as the wind, as untouchable as the wind, as beautiful as the wind.

And now listen to the story of Koro, and of Mana, the woman he loved.

And old Sandu, the Gipsy story-teller, too Gipsy to stay even with Gipsies, having assured himself of the attention of the hundred swarthy faces of the circle around the camp-fire burning brightly in the moonlit night on the wooded shores of the Danube, told the story of Koro:

You know Koro. I have seen him the other day in the desert of Yalomitza. You remember him—tall and straight as an arrow, with fiery eyes and commanding voice. Koro, who could laugh louder than he could sing. Koro of a thousand loves, and no hatred. Koro who, alone, after the cholera had killed most of his tribe, went riding his young stallion with no gun to defend himself, and no whip to spur his horse, to gather the stray Gipsies of the roads. He welded them into one of the strongest Tchiatras (caravans) anywhere between the Danube and the Carpathians between the Danube and the Black Sea— between the Prut and the Dniester rivers. Straylings from everywhere no longer looked at one another as enemies. Men and women with Tartar blood in their veins and Hungarian and Russian and peasant blood rushing through them, sheep, wolves, doves and serpents, long-legged and short-limbed Lazes without necks and bullet-like heads, and Bulgars with shoulders as wide as the axle of this carriage upon limbs so short they seemed to crawl when they walked, were all welded into one large caravan.

And he ruled them, Koro, without whip and without gun—with a smile at the right time and a stern look, softened by a witty word. And it seemed Koro would never come to grief. Because of the love of the people for him, because of the sharpness of his own mind—because he knew human weakness and knew where the soul of man and woman was most deeply hidden, and knew how and where to reach it.

But weep now. I have seen Koro in the desert of Yalomitza. The life in his eyes has gone out. There is no ring in his voice, it has died out. And tho his lips still strive after a smile, they open slowly and heavily, like the lips of a child before it has learned to smile. And to forget is a thousand times worse than not to know. His back is bent, his shoulders slump, his knees sag. Alone he sits near the small creek running through the desert and looks into the gurgling narrow stream that cuts through like a steel knife the glittering sands of the bed of the river. Weep—for Koro, tho still alive, is dead! A word has killed him. One lone word not uttered by a woman has done what neither knife nor bullet had once been able to do.

After Koro had assembled close to two hundred stray wagons from all over the country, he brought them down to the desert of Yalomitza to winter there. There were many girls of marriageable age in the camp, there were many young men who played the violin and sang, and the nights were long.

Before the snow had fallen, the tent wagons had been spread into wide circles, an outer and an inner one. Then the wheels were buried in the ground up to the

axle to protect them against the winds of the winter.
And between the two rows of wagons they stretched
canvas, underneath which was prepared the winter
quarters for the horses. Then those who had smaller
children dug holes into the ground to protect themselves from the cold. And Koro supervized what was
being done, and he saw to it that it was being done
with joy and song and laughter among the men, so
that they should touch hands while they worked and
become friends.

When the first heavy snow had fallen, they filled the
empty space under the wagons with it, and packed it
solid so that the wind should not blow underneath.
There was fodder for the horses and food enough for
the caravan to last the whole winter. Then Koro
brought new sets of strings for the violins from
Calarasi. For he wished a gay winter; one from which
both horses and men should come out stronger than
they had gone in; with eager eyes and arms aching
for work.

The first Sunday night Pablo, the Gitana from Spain,
who had come to the country God knows how and
why, sang one of the songs of his people. Then the
other men and women sang songs of their own people,
and sang them each twice and three times so that the
others should also learn them. Koro returned to his
tent, in which he lived alone, for his wife had died not
long before. He was happy and satisfied that that
night of song had welded his people together more
than they had been before.

The following evening there were several wrestling-
matches, in which men tried their strength and methods
of throwing one another. The Bulgars tried to break
the back of their fighting partners by winding their

long arms under the shoulders and pressing their chins against the man in the opposite direction. The long-limbed Magyars twined their legs around those of their antagonists until they looked like snakes that had rolled one in another.

And so the men learned from one another. And when things had gone well for a long time Koro began to think a little more of himself. He was alone. He was forty, and much younger than his age. So he began to look around for a wife unto himself from among the people he had assembled. And he measured the women not by what his wife had been before she died, for she had been ill a long time, but what she had been when he had first known her.

And at first it seemed to him there was none that could be as much or more to him. He talked to the young maidens in a friendly way, read hope in their eyes—hope and yielding. For tho he was forty, he was a chief. And he was strong and wise.

When the mothers of the girls told them that it was ill to have a man three times one's age be the father of one's children, each one answered that surely one had no right to expect Koro to marry a woman of his own age! Why, the "Barrosan" was younger than the youngest. He could outdance any one in the tribe. He could remain the last one on his feet when all the others would, toward morning, fall down of exhaustion. And there was not a single man he could not down in a wrestling-match. They were certain of that.

Week passed week. Snowstorms became heavier and more prolonged. Mountains of snow were raised by the wind and thrown from one place to another, as if they were only little balls. Dance succeeded dance, and Sunday night succeeded Sunday night, and

still Koro had not seen the one he desired for a wife.
The older men told stories of their own lives and of
their own heroes to one another and there was not a
Sunday in which Koro was not called upon to celebrate
a wedding among the younger people.

They rejoiced and sang, and welded together like
one—and still Koro had not chosen a wife unto
himself. Every time he looked at a new bride before
the chosen one scratched her wrist to bring blood, and
before he tied their hands together so that the blood
should mingle, and be pronounced man and wife, Koro
looked at the bride and questioned himself whether
she might have been the one he wanted.

And loveless nights Koro passed in his tent. There
were many women who would have willingly shared
his tent for a night. He made believe he did not
understand their gestures and the glances in their eyes.

Then one day, from the circle around the camp-fire
under the canvas between the two wagons, there stepped
out a young girl whose white hand was held tightly by
a half-breed young Tartar.

"That we be married," the young man asked of
Koro. Koro smiled his good smiles upon them—but
an instant later a tremor passed through his body.
Why had he overlooked that girl? True, she was
young, he doubted whether she had already seen her
sixteenth summer, but there was something ripe and
full about her face, and her eyes opened as she looked
at Koro, telling him that she was wise in the ways
of men. She was tall and straight-limbed. And
Koro could not take his eyes off her throat and her
neck, so beautifully they were shaped and so tempting
did the lines go down to part her breasts, like twin
hills of snow, that showed under the thin white nome-

spun shirt she was wearing. She held her head thrust
backward, and her slightly arched nose was lit by
the strong light that came from her eyes. Why hadn't
he seen her before? Koro asked himself. He shook
himself together and looked at the young man. He
had seen him before, and he realized now how little
he had liked him. There was something ugly under the
smirk of the thick lips of the Tartar boy. Why had
she chosen him?

It had never taken Koro so long to answer a couple
who wanted to be married. And the young girl looked
into his eyes, and knew why Koro hesitated so long.
Her eyes spoke as she looked at him, and they said:
"Why haven't you seen me till now?"
Suddenly Koro whipped out his long blade from the
top of his boot. He closed one eye to look at the
keenness of the edge, and he dug just a little too deep
into the wrist of the young man; for there was a
slight whimper on the part of the bullet-headed boy.
When the blood drops had come to the surface, Koro
handed the boy the knife, that he should bleed the
wrist of the girl for the marriage ceremony. Koro
watched him and it seemed to him that the boy also
dug a little too deep into the girl's flesh. Koro's
fingers curved ready to tear the young man's throat.
But the bride never whimpered. Her wrist was tied
to that of Achmet's so that the blood should mingle,
and Koro called them man and wife.
People sang and danced and drank. Koro talked and
danced and sang with them. Yet there was a curtain
between him and the people. He saw them indistinctly.
The colors of their clothes mingled together and danced
before his eyes and their voice rang shrilly, while

the wind flopped the canvas overhead. Their limbs twined and untwined themselves in the wild dances that followed. Once and again Koro was dragged into the midst and asked to dance with the bride. And so slender and yielding was her body to his it aroused all his passions, and he was angry at himself for looking with such displeasure at the Tartar boy who had married her. And he was angry at himself for not having seen her before. He must have passed her by a hundred times. Why hadn't he seen her? Now she was another man's wife. Another man's wife was another man's wife. And he was Koro the ruler. He could not do what he did not want other people of his tribe to do.

Toward the morning when the groom and the bride had been sent hand in hand and blindfolded to find their tent, after they had been spun around so as to lose their direction, Koro let the others amuse themselves watching them stumble over wheels and being thrown head foremost over young men lying on their fours. For hours afterward Koro could hear the camp rock with laughter. Once they even stumbled upon his own tent wagon. Soon after that had happened rose a loud and slow song. The bride and the groom had found their own tent wagon. Deep silence followed after that.

The storm shook the two hundred wagons, which squeaked and squealed and groaned like so many wrestlers upon the ground before they are being turned over on their backs. A still wider circle—a pack of wolves sat hunched with their hungry red tongues sticking out, wagging and waiting for prey and food.

So, many weeks passed and there were many other weddings which Koro celebrated. And tho he looked a little closer now to the women of the tribe than he had looked before, he never saw one that aroused him as much as Mana.

And drink as hard as he drank, and work as hard as he worked—taking upon himself more work than three men could do—at night when he was alone the image of Mana standing before him looking into his eyes as he married her to that bullet-headed Tartar boy rose before his eyes.

He saw very little of her during the next four weeks, for as was the custom among the Tartar Gipsies, bride and groom were left alone. Food and drink were brought to their tent, and they only seldom stuck their heads out. For it is the belief of those people that like oxen—paired for the first time to a yoke, who fight before they have adjusted themselves to the same pace, and even break the yoke—men and women should be left alone until they have adjusted themselves to one another.

But soon afterward rumors began to come to Koro that all was not well within Achmet's tent. Men had heard cries in the night, and tho Mana appeared seemingly as gay as all the others in the tents of women, the other women were not short to notice that her gaiety was only an apparent one. Mana's mother asked her with tears in her eyes to tell her how Achmet behaved toward her. But Mana laughed and answered:

"If there is anybody to complain, Achmet has more to complain of than I have."

But then, no one had any right to mix in the affairs within a tent.

One day Koro saw Achmet and it seemed to him that

the boy looked at him almost provokingly. Koro did not know that there probably had been a strange look in his own eyes when he had answered Achmet's greeting.

A few days later Koro sent Achmet to the village to buy salt; for they had run out of it. He stood, Koro, at the flap of his own tent, while Achmet had gone to his, and listened—and it seemed to him that he heard even then a soft smothered cry. A tremor passed through the big body. That a man could be so cruel to one so beautiful, that youth could be so stupid as to torture some one who deserved so much to be loved!

The whole afternoon Koro waited for Mana to come to him, to talk to him. He knew that there were many things she wanted to tell him. But she didn't come. Achmet returned from the errand. And again Koro heard smothered cries from within the tent. He grabbed the short handle of his long leather-plaited whip and was ready to spring to the girl's defense. But a man's tent is a man's tent—and a man's wife is a man's wife. Why should he care? There were other men who did likewise to their women. All the Tartar youths had such cursed habits. They all beat their women even the day after the wedding!

The following day and the following day people of Koro's kind, pure-blooded Gipsies, came shaking their heads dolefully. They seemed more concerned with Mana's fate than with the fate of the other girls. And Mana's father's brother came to Koro to tell him that she had come to talk. But isn't a man's tent a man's tent? he asked.

"It is," Koro answered. "But are they men?"

Mana's uncle shrugged his shoulders and left. He had hardly gone when Mana came rushing to Koro's tent. She fell in a heap before him. Achmet had beaten her mercilessly with a whip until the tongue had slashed through the clothing she wore. She looked at the old man for help, as tho she mutely accused him for what had happened to her. Then something strange happened within Koro. Instead of rushing out to punish the youth he lifted the young woman to his cot, and looked for the salves he had in his trunk. Her whole body was streaked with blue welts, as thick as a finger, that ran from her limbs to her neck like serpents that were strangling her. A number of women had come running to Koro's tent. Tears were blinding him as he applied salves upon the wounded body. One of the women tried to replace Koro at the salving of Mana's body.

"Let him do it—his fingers are softer than yours and tenderer," Mana cried.

When he had salved her, he was wounded himself. That a man could maltreat so beautiful a body! Koro walked out of the tent. Achmet stood in a circle surrounded by people of his own kind, young and old. What did Koro mean by taking the woman of another man into his tent? What business had he with her? He should have driven her out of it, or called her man to take her away the minute she appeared. She was the man's woman, and he, he alone, had rights upon her. And so they yelled:

"And isn't a man's tent a man's tent?"

To which Koro answered:

"It is, but is he a man?"

And then Koro talked. There was no hatred in his heart against these young men.

All of them, he knew, were torturing their wives. There was no hatred in his breast even against Achmet. And it was merely the stupidity of youth and bad habits that made him so sad. The arrogance of youth, which blinded them to the treasures they possessed. And it was of that which he spoke to them.

"And as to returning Mana to your tent, Achmet, she will have to ask me to do that. It isn't I who would tell her to return to you. I have seen what you have done to her."

Upon that he rose and turned his back on them to go back to his tent from where he heard the soft moaning of Mana. He had only gone a few steps when a knife grazed his ears and he had to duck other knives flying past him. Koro reached his tent bleeding from several places in his arms and legs.

"Be still," he told Mana, and taking the gun from the corner he appeared before the pack closing in on him. There were a good many men of his own kin that had joined the Tartar half-breed to defend the inviolate right of the Gipsy in his tent. They howled and shrieked. Koro was ready to shoot.

"I want an hour's council with myself, before I decide what is right or wrong. Pick your knives from off the ground and go to your own tents. Come back in an hour and what I shall decide will be decided."

There was a short parley between the people and then Achmet said:

"One hour then, Koro."

Koro returned to his tent, from where he drove out the women that had assembled, and remained alone with Mana. After looking longingly in her eyes he asked:

"Why have you come to me?"

"Because of the look in your eyes when Achmet dug deeper than was necessary in my wrist at the wedding."

No other words were necessary between them.

"Why has he tortured you?" Koro asked.

"You never would, Koro," Mana said, remarking for the first time that he was bleeding.

"Koro, you are bleeding."

He hushed her. "It is nothing," he answered.

"Why have you stood it so long?"

She did not answer.

He looked at the welts on the girl's body. They had turned from blue to brown and from brown to black, circling and entwining one another. There was silence between them for a few moments, and then Mana said:

"You will never love me, Koro—my body has been torn to shreds."

Koro buried his head tenderly in the girl's arm, and his huge frame shook with sobs.

"I shall love you forever—and I shall heal your wounds with my love. I thank the moon and the sun for having given you first to that savage, so that you should think of coming to me."

And his wisdom and his quietness flowed into the girl's own body and mind, and she became as one with him merely by looking at him.

"And what now?" she asked.

"In a few hours you will come with me, alone or with those who will care to come with us. And if we are not torn by the wolves on the way or if I am not killed before, we shall go far away from here."

Even before the hour was up most of the men had assembled in front of Koro's tent screaming. Koro came out. The youth had ranged itself on one side— dogged and fierce, without heart and without understanding. The older men were standing apart.

"She refuses to go to your tent, Achmet," Koro announced, holding his gun ready.

"Then we shall take her."

A dozen men sprang to Koro's defense in the next moment—not because they thought he was right, but because he was their chief. Shrieks and screams pierced the air.

Before the sun had moved one finger's length upon the sky, there were many splotches of blood on the white snow, and the wolves had drawn closer, seeing that the men were occupied in killing one another instead of protecting themselves from them. A few more of the older men joined Koro's side, and when the few shots each one possessed had found their mark, the men grabbed their knives from the top-boots, and fought one another with teeth and steel. The women shrieked at the top of their voices and the children looked on, not understanding what was happening. They were all pressing from behind and from the front to get Koro away from his tent wagon. Mana looked through a hole in the canvas at what was going on.

And suddenly the wolves who had been surrounding the camp for many days, attracted now by the odor of blood and by the men fallen to the ground, came rushing and threw themselves upon the wounded and the dead. Instantly the Gipsies forgot their quarrel and turned to drive the wild beasts off.

Koro leaped upon his horse with the wounded woman

wrapped in fur skins in front of him and drove off
and away.

By the time they reached the next village it was
night. Mana, whose eyes seemed to have grown
much larger, was stretched out peacefully like one
who has come out from a good dream after a long
sickness and looked at him. They were in the hut of
a friend of Koro's on whom he could rely to defend
him should the others find them.

And so day after day passed, and night after night,
during which Koro salved the body of the woman.

"Your hands are even more healing than the salve,"
she said to him again and again. "I shall be sorry to
get well."

And more even than his hands it was the love and
warmth that emanated from him as he talked to her
that got her better. His caresses drove the welts in
and melted the blood that had coagulated. And then
one night Mana said:

"You love me not."

Koro kissed her tenderly.

"Perhaps it is because I have been tender with
you, Mana, that you think *you* love me. I want you
to get well first. When your body is as beautiful and
wholesome as it had been be.......chmet had ever
seen it, then you shall decide whether you want my
love."

She wondered at his kind wisdom, for she knew how
much he loved her, and yet she wished he was not so
wise. She wished he showed a little more impatience,
so that she might later call him to account.

The rest of the Winter Koro salved her morning and
evenings. When Spring came, and there was no longer

a single sign of the tortures the other one had inflicted upon her, Koro rode with her into Calarasi among his own people and took her into his tent wagon as his wife. And it was at Calarasi that he heard that the people he had gathered from everywhere to weld them together had again spread all over the country. And it was in Calarasi that he had heard of the fight that followed after he had left them and after they had driven off the wolves. Every wagon had been broken and many of the men and horses had been killed. Each one wanted to take more than he had brought with him. The stronger ones robbed the weaker ones. And as the strangers were more numerous than the group of full-blooded Gipsies, Koro's people suffered defeat. And Koro thought it very strange that all the misfortunes of his own people should touch him so very lightly when they told him about it. He wondered—but then he was so happy!

Mana had rejuvenated him, while she had become much mellower. Yet he felt she desired him to be harsh with her. He talked to her.

"Why should you want pain?" he asked her. "Isn't your body a thousand times more beautiful now than it had been with the ugly signs upon it?"

And then she would touch his beard as if she were trying to caress some pain away from him.

"It is, Koro. You have kissed my wounds away. You have caressed my pains away."

And what he thought she thought, and what he said she repeated to the others, not even knowing that it wasn't she who had thought it first and that it wasn't she who had said it first.

And so that people Koro had again gathered about him began to speak of her wisdom and of her knowl-

edge. "That one so young should know so much!"
they said.

Koro worried over the youths that were joining
his tribe. But he realized soon how little attention
Mana paid to them. She laughed and scoffed at them.
Day after day she grew more beautiful. And her
eyes lit up with a light that was not wholly hers.
And her voice sang songs that were not hers. Even
Koro did not know how much of himself she reflected.

And so spring and summer went away, with the
caravan becoming larger and larger and the reputation
of Mana spreading farther and farther.

Late that fall, Koro and his people arrived at the
Black Sea, where they camped for the large fair at
Constanza. And there they met a small tribe of
Gipsies which traveled alone, without aim and without
leader. After they had joined Koro's caravan Mana
remarked that there were many more musicians among
them than among the others. And there were several
wise old men among them who loved to sit around the
camp-fire and give of their wisdom and tell tales. And
then Mana, who had listened so much to the wisdom
of Koro while she had been with him, would frequently
say something that startled the older men. And every
time she did so she met the eyes of Koro as if he
told her, "You are pluming yourself with my feathers."
And so she began to avoid the older men and went
instead to talk and sing with the younger ones who
usually formed a group apart from the others, with
Koro seldom in their midst.

And among the younger men was one Gregory. And
it seemed to Koro that he resembled Achmet. Gregory
followed every movement of Mana with his eyes, and

every time Gregory looked at her she looked at him. Koro could not understand why she found more pleasure in his company than in the company of the other youths in the caravan. Koro felt he was younger than all of them—he could outdance and outsing any of them. He could wrestle any one of them down. But because he could do all these things, because he was the master, he never felt it necessary to show the others what he could do. Only young men, uncertain of themselves, are continually proving to one another their valor and their strength, really only giving proof of the weakness of their bodies and minds.

And then, after a while, Koro began to feel how Mana was slipping from him. Even when he had his arms about her, even when he had her head resting on his shoulder, he felt that she was far away—that a more important part of her was not near him. He loved her with greater passion and greater abandon, yet he felt her slipping. And so he became sadder. And because he was sad she grew further away from him.

Day succeeded day and the camp became gayer every evening, not a sun setting without some entertainment. Laughter and song echoed till late into the night into Koro's tent. He could hear Mana's laugh. She was always with them. When she returned to the tent, however, her face was sad.

And then one morning, still warm from Koro's embrace, she told him:

"Gregory loves me," and she looked at her man's eyes.

He did not answer, waiting for her to say more. So she repeated:

"I have said, Gregory loves me."

"I have heard this," he answered. "Why shouldn't he? There are many others in the camp who love you. You are beautiful."

"Are you going to kill him because he loves me?"

"No," he answered. "I should have to kill so many others."

She turned around fiercely:

"And I love him."

Koro closed his eyes; everything within him had been blinded.

"He is strong, and is willing to fight for me. And he is young."

Koro was hardly able to contain the fury that seized him. He wished he was stupid enough to strike her. But he mastered himself and said softly:

"And can I not outdance him, and am I not stronger than he is?"

"Then why don't you ever dance—or ever wrestle?"

"It is because I know that I can do these things better than they can that I don't do them."

"And will you fight him?"

"No," Koro said.

A moment later he took her wrist into his hand and said:

"Look at him—see how much he resembles Achmet."

"He does resemble Achmet," she said as if she had never thought of that.

"He will be as cruel to you as the other has been."

"Ah," Mana, answered "I have grown wiser since. Now I understand that every time he whipped me it was because of his own weakness. Every time he was cruel to me it was because of his own fear of me. But you—you who never want to dance because you can dance, and never want to wrestle because you can wrestle, and never want to whip me because of your certainty that no one can take me away from you—you have humiliated me! Because of your certainty that you can win you are losing!"

Koro looked at her and understood all that she might have told him and didn't. It was in her eyes, in the timber of her voice.

"You are old, Koro."

And at the moment he felt as if one hundred years had come down upon him—a hundred unlived years—that many others had lived in pain and suffering which now weighed down upon his shoulders. It was the wisdom of woman to take with the right hand from one and give with the left hand to another. The wisdom of woman, who knows that she can rule better by giving than by taking. And she destroyed in Koro what he might have still given some one else. She destroyed it with the look in her eyes, with the timber of her voice. Youth prefers to be tortured by youth. All Koro's tenderness and love could not outweigh the youth of Gregory.

And then having left him, she went to the other one —some one who had yet much to prove and to learn, some one who would listen to her wisdom—the wisdom borrowed from Koro—which he had given because he loved and which she had taken to make herself loved by others.

That night Koro left for the wilderness of the desert.

Gregory and Mana are ruling the tribe now.

You can hear of her wisdom from one end of the country to the other. They wonder that a woman so beautiful and so wise should let herself be treated so cruelly by Gregory, who is neither handsome nor wise.

And now, hey, ho! Sing again the song of the

north wind. It comes from nowhere. Sing again the song of the wisdom of woman—she comes from nowhere. She is wind fashioned into flesh and bone. As stron as the wind. As untouchable as the wind. As beautiful as the wind. And sing also the song of Youth. Youth to Youth is the end of all wisdom.

I'M A FOOL

By SHERWOOD ANDERSON

It was a hard jolt for me, one of the most bitterest
I ever had to face. And it all came about through
my own foolishness too. Even yet, sometimes, when
I think of it, I want to cry or swear or kick myself.
Perhaps, even now, after all this time, there will be a
kind of satisfaction in making myself look cheap by
telling of it.

It began at three o'clock one October afternoon as I
sat in the grand stand at the fall trotting and pacing
meet at Sandusky, Ohio.

To tell the truth, I felt a little foolish that I should
be sitting in the grand stand at all. During the summer before I had left my home town with Harry
Whitehead and, with a nigger named Burt, had taken
a job as swipe with one of the two horses Harry
was campaigning through the fall race meets that year.
Mother cried and my sister Mildred, who wanted to
get a job as a school teacher in our town that fall,
stormed and scolded about the house all during the
week before I left. They both thought it something
disgraceful that one of our family should take a
place as a swipe with race horses. I've an idea Mildred
thought my taking the place would stand in the way

of her getting the job she'd been working so long for.

But after all I had to work and there was no other work to be got. A big lumbering fellow of nineteen couldn't just hang around the house and I had got too big to mow people's lawns and sell newspapers. Little chaps who could get next to people's sympathies by their sizes were always getting jobs away from me. There was one fellow who kept saying to everyone who wanted a lawn mowed or a cistern cleaned, that he was saving money to work his way through college, and I used to lay awake nights thinking up ways to injure him without being found out. I kept thinking of wagons running over him and bricks falling on his head as he walked along the street. But never mind him.

I got the place with Harry and I liked Burt fine. We got along splendid together. He was a big nigger with a lazy sprawling body and soft kind eyes, and when it came to a fight he could hit like Jack Johnson. He had Bucephalus, a big black pacing stallion that could do 2.09 or 2.10 if he had to, and I had a little gelding named Doctor Fritz that never lost a race all fall when Harry wanted him to win.

We set out from home late in July in a box car with the two horses and after that, until late November, we kept moving along to the race meets and the fairs. It was a peachy time for me, I'll say that. Sometimes, now, I think that boys who are raised regular in houses, and never have a fine nigger like Burt for best friend, and go to high schools and college, and never steal anything or get drunk a little, or learn to swear from fellows who know how, or come walking up in front of a grand stand in their shirt sleeves and with dirty horsey pants on when the races are going on and the grand stand is full of people all dressed up—What's the use talking about it? Such fellows don't know nothing at all. They've never had no opportunity.

But I did. Burt taught me how to rub down a horse and put the bandages on after a race and steam a horse out and a lot of valuable things for any man to know. He could wrap a bandage on a horse's leg so smooth that if it had been the same color you would think it was his skin, and I guess he'd have been a big driver too and got to the top like Murphy and Walter Cox and the others if he hadn't been black.

Gee whizz, it was fun. You got to a county seat down maybe, say, on a Saturday or Sunday, and the fair began the next Tuesday and lasted until Friday afternoon. Doctor Fritz would be, say, in the 2.25 trot on Tuesday afternoon and on Thursday afternoon Bucephalus would knock 'em cold in the "free-for-all" pace. It left you a lot of time to hang around and listen to horse talk, and see Burt knock some yap cold that got too gay, and you'd find out about horses and men and pick up a lot of stuff you could use all the rest of your life if you had some sense and salted down what you heard and felt and saw.

And then at the end of the week when the race meet was over, and Harry had run home to tend up to his livery stable business, you and Burt hitched the two horses to carts and drove slow and steady across country to the place for the next meeting so as to not over-heat the horses, etc., etc., you know.

Gee whizz, gosh amighty, the nice hickorynut and beech-nut and oaks and other kinds of trees along the roads, all brown and red, and the good smells, and Burt singing a song that was called Deep River, and the

country girls at the windows of houses and everything
You can stick your colleges up your nose for all me. I
guess I know where I got my education.

Why, one of those little burgs of towns you come
to on the way, say now, on a Saturday afternoon, and
Burt says, "let's lay up here." And you did.

And you took the horses to a livery stable and fed
them and you got your good clothes out of a box
and put them on.

And the town was full of farmers gaping, because
they could see you were race horse people, and the
kids maybe never see a nigger before and was afraid
and run away when the two of us walked down their
main street.

And that was before prohibition and all that foolishness, and so you went into a saloon, the two of
you, and all the yaps come and stood around, and there
was always someone pretended he was horsey and
knew things and spoke up and began asking questions,
and all you did was to lie and lie all you could about
what horses you had, and I said I owned them, and
then some fellow said, "Will you have a drink of
whisky?" and Burt knocked his eye out the way he
could say, offhand like, "Oh, well, all right, I'm agreeable to a little nip. I'll split a quart with you." Gee
whizz.

But that isn't what I want to tell my story about.
We got home late in November and I promised mother
I'd quit the race horses for good. There's a lot of
things you've got to promise a mother because she
don't know any better.

And so, there not being any work in our town any
more than when I left there to go to the races, I went
off to Sandusky and got a pretty good place taking

care of the horses for a man who owned a teaming and delivery and storage business there. It was a pretty good place with good eats and a day off each week and sleeping on a cot in the big barn, and mostly just shoveling in hay and oats to a lot of big good-enough skates of horses that couldn't have trotted a race with a toad. I wasn't dissatisfied and I could send money home.

And then, as I started to tell you, the fall races come to Sandusky and I got the day off and I went. I left the job at noon and had on my good clothes and my new brown derby hat I'd just bought the Saturday before, and a stand-up collar.

First of all I went downtown and walked about with the dudes. I've always thought to myself, "put up a good front," and so I did it. I had forty dollars in my pocket and so I went into the West House, a big hotel, and walked up to the cigar stand. "Give me three twenty-five cent cigars," I said. There was a lot of horse men and strangers and dressed-up people from other towns standing around in the lobby and in the bar, and I mingled amongst them. In the bar there was a fellow with a cane and a Windsor tie on, that it made me sick to look at him. I like a man to be a man and dress up, but not to go put on that kind of airs. So I pushed him aside, kind of rough, and had me a drink of whisky. And then he looked at me as tho he thought maybe he'd get gay, but he changed his mind and didn't say anything. And then I had another drink of whisky, just to show him something, and went out and had a hack out to the races all to myself, and when I got there I bought myself the best seat i could get up in the grand

stand, but didn't go in for any of these boxes. That's
putting on too many airs.

And so there I was, sitting up in the grand stand
as gay as you please and looking down on the swipes
coming out with their horses and with their dirty
horsey pants on and the horse blankets swung over
their shoulders same as I had been doing all the year
before. I liked one thing about the same as the other,
sitting up there and feeling grand and being down there
and looking up at the yaps and feeling grander and
more important too. One thing's about as good as
another if you take it just right. I've often said
that.

Well, right in front of me, in the grand stand that
day, there was a fellow with a couple of girls and they
was about my age. The young fellow was a nice guy
all right. He was the kind maybe that goes to college
and then comes to be a lawyer or maybe a newspaper
editor or something like that, but he wasn't stuck on
himself. There are some of that kind are all right,
and he was one of the ones.

He had his sister with him and another girl and the
sister looked around over his shoulder, accidental at
first, not intending to start anything—she wasn't that
kind—and her eyes and mine happened to meet.

You know how it is. Gee, she was a peach. She
had on a soft dress, kind of a blue stuff and it looked
carelessly made, but was well sewed and made and
everything. I knew that much. I blushed when she
looked right at me and so did she. She was the nicest
girl I've ever seen in my life. She wasn't stuck on
herself and she could talk proper grammar without
being like a school teacher or something like that.
What I mean is, she was O.K. I think maybe her

father was well-to-do, but not rich to make her chesty because she was his daughter, as some are. Maybe he owned a drug store or a dry goods store in their home town, or something like that. She never told me and I never asked.

My own people are all O.K. too, when you come to that. My grandfather was Welsh and over in the old country, in Wales he was—but never mind that.

The first heat of the first race come off and the young fellow setting there with the two girls left them and went down to make a bet. I knew what he was up to, but he didn't talk big and noisy and let everyone around know he was a sport, as some do. He wasn't that kind. Well, he come back and I heard him tell the two girls what horse he'd bet on, and when the heat was trotted they all half got to their feet and acted in the excited, sweaty way people do when they've got money down on a race, and the horse they bet on is up there pretty close at the end, and they think maybe he'll come on with a rush, but he never does because he hasn't got the old juice in him, come right down to it.

And then, pretty soon, the horses came out for the 2.18 pace and there was a horse in it I knew. He was a horse Bob French had in his string, but Bob didn't own him. He was a horse owned by a Mr. Mathers down at Marietta, Ohio.

This Mr. Mathers had a lot of money and owned some coal mines or something, and he had a swell place out in the country, and he was stuck on race horses, but was a Presbyterian or something, and I think more than likely his wife was one, too, maybe a stiffer one than himself. So he never raced his horses hisself, and the story round the Ohio race tracks

was that when one of his horses got ready to go to
the races he turned him over to Bob French and pretended to his wife he was sold.

. So Bob had the horses and he did pretty much as
he pleased and you can't blame Bob, at least, I never
did. Sometimes he was out to win and sometimes he
wasn't. I never cared much about that when I was
swiping a horse. What I did want to know was that
my horse had the speed and could go out in front if
you wanted him to.

And, as I'm telling you, there was Bob in this race
with one of Mr. Mathers' horses, was named "About
Ben Ahem" or something like that, and was fast as a
streak. He was a gelding and had a mark of 2.21, but
could step in .08 or .09.

Because when Burt and I were out, as I've told
you, the year before, there was a nigger Burt knew,
worked for Mr. Mathers, and we went out there one
day when we didn't have no race on at the Marietta
Fair and our boss Harry was gone home.

And so everyone was gone to the fair but just this
one nigger, and he took us all through Mr. Mathers'
swell house and he and Burt tapped a bottle of wine
Mr. Mathers had hid in his bedroom, back in a closet,
without his wife knowing, and he showed us this Ahem
horse. Burt was always stuck on being a driver, but
didn't have much chance to get to the top, being a
nigger, and he and the other nigger gulped that whole
bottle of wine and Burt got a little lit up.

So the nigger let Burt take this About Ben Ahem
and step him a mile in a track Mr. Mathers had all to
himself, right there on the farm. And Mr. Mathers
had one child, a daughter, kinda sick and not very

good looking, and she came home and we had to nustle
and get About Ben Ahem stuck back in the barn.

I'm only telling you to get everything straight. At
Sandusky, that afternoon I was at the fair, this young
fellow with the two girls was fussed, being with the
girls and losing his bet. You know how a fellow is
that way. One of them was his girl and the other
his sister. I had figured that out.

"Gee whizz," I says to myself, "I'm going to give
him the dope."

He was mighty nice when I touched him on the
shoulder. He and the girls were nice to me right from
the start and clear to the end. I'm not blaming them.

And so he leaned back and I gave him the dope on
About Ben Ahem. "Don't bet a cent on this first heat
because he'll go like an oxen hitched to a plow,
but when the first heat is over go right down and lay
on your pile." That's what I told him.

Well, I never saw a fellow treat any one sweller.
There was a fat man sitting beside the little girl that
had looked at me twice by this time, and _ at her, and
both blushing, and what did he do but have the nerve
to turn and ask the fat man to get up and change
places with me so I could set with his crowd.

Gee whizz, amighty. There I was. What a chump
I was to go and get gay up there in the West House
bar, and just because that dude was standing there
with a cane and that kind of a necktie on, to go and
get all balled up and drink that whisky, just to
show off.

Of course she would know, me setting right beside
her and letting her smell of my breath. I could
have kicked myself right down out of that grand stand
and all around that race track and made a faster

record than most of the skates of horses they had there that year.

Because that girl wasn't any mutt of a girl. What wouldn't I have give right then for a stick of chewing gum to chew, or a lozenger, or some licorice, or most anything. I was glad I had those twenty-five cent cigars in my pocket, and right away I give that fellow one and lit one myself. Then that fat man got up and we changed places and there I was plunked right down beside her.

They introduced themselves, and the fellow's best girl he had with him, was named Miss Elinor Woodbury, and her father was a manufacturer of barrels from a place called Tiffin, Ohio. And the fellow himself was named Wilbur Wessen and his sister was Miss Lucy Wessen.

I suppose it was their having such swell names got me off my trolley. A fellow, just because he has been a swipe with a race horse, and works taking care of horses for a man in the teaming, delivery and storage business, isn't any better or worse than any one else. I've often thought that, and said it, too.

But you know how a fellow is. There's something in that kind of nice clothes, and the kind of nice eyes she had, and the way she had looked at me, awhile before, over her brother's shoulder, and me looking back at her, and both of us blushing.

I couldn't show her up for a boob, could I?

I made a fool of myself, that's what I did. I said my name was Walter Mathers from Marietta, Ohio, and then I told all three of them the smashingest lie you ever heard. What I said was that my father owned the horse About Ben Ahem, and that he had let him out to this Bob French for racing purposes,

because our family was proud and had never gone
into racing that way, in our own name, I mean. Then
I had got started and they were all leaning over and
listening, and Miss Lucy Wessen's eyes were shining,
and I went the whole hog.

I told about our place down at Marietta, and about
the big stables and the grand brick house we had on
a hill, up above the Ohio River, but I knew enough
not to do it in no bragging way. What I did was to
start things and then let them drag the rest out of me.
I acted just as reluctant to tell as I could. Our family
hasn't got any barrel factory, and, since I've known
us, we've always been pretty poor, but not asking
anything of anyone at that, and my grandfather, over
in Wales—but never mind that.

We set there talking like we had known each other
for years and years, and I went and told them that
my father had been expecting maybe this Bob French
wasn't on the square, and had sent me up to Sandusky on the sly to find out what I could.

And I bluffed it through. I had found out all about
the 2.18 pace in which About Ben Ahem was to start.

I said he would lose the first heat by pacing like
a lame cow and then he would come back and skin 'em
alive after that. And to back up what I said I took
thirty dollars out of my pocket and handed it to
Mr. Wilbur Wessen and asked him would he mind,
after the first heat, to go down and place it on About
Ben Ahem for whatever odds he could get. What I
said was that I didn't want Bob French to see me and
none of the swipes.

Sure enough the first heat come off and About
Ben Ahem went off his stride, up the back stretch,
and looked like a wooden horse or a sick one, and

come in to be last. Then this Wilbur Wessen went
down to the betting place under the grand stand and
there I was with the two girls, and when that Miss
Woodbury was looking the other way once, Lucy
Wessen kinda, with her shoulder you know, kinda
touched me. Not just tucking down, I don't mean.
You know how a woman can do. They get close, but
not getting gay either. You know what they do. Gee
whizz.

And then they give me a jolt. What they had done
when I didn't know, was to get together, and they had
decided Wilbur Wessen would bet fifty dollars, and
the two girls had gone and put in ten dollars each of
their own money, too. I was sick then, but I was
sicker later.

About the gelding, About Ben Ahem, and their win-
ning their money, I wasn't worried a lot about that.
It come out O.K. Ahem stepped the next three heats
like a bushel of spoiled eggs going to market before
they could be found out, and Wilbur Wessen had got
nine to two for the money. There was something
else eating at me.

Because Wilbur come back after he had bet the
money, and after that he spent most of his time
talking to that Miss Woodbury, and Lucy Wessen and
I was left alone together like on a desert island. Gee,
if I'd only been on the square or if there had been
any way of getting myself on the square. There ain't
any Walter Mathers, like I said to her and them, and
there hasn't ever been one, but if there was, I bet I'd
go to Marietta, Ohio, and shoot him tomorrow.

There I was, big boob that I am. Pretty soon the
race was over, and Wilbur had gone down and col-
lected our money, and we had a hack downtown, and

he stood us a swell dinner at the West House, and a
bottle of champagne beside.

And I was with that girl and she wasn't saying much,
and I wasn't saying much either. One thing I know.
She wasn't stuck on me because of the lie about my
father being rich and all that. There's a way you
know. . . . Craps amighty. There's a kind of girl
you see just once in your life, and if you don't get
busy and make hay then you're gone for good and all
and might as well go jump off a bridge. They give
you a look from inside of them somewhere, and it
ain't no vamping, and what it means is—you want that
girl to be your wife, and you want nice things around
her like flowers and swell clothes, and you want her
to have the kids you're going to have, and you want
good music played and no ragtime. Gee whizz.

There's a place over near Sandusky, across a kind
of bay, and it's called Cedar Point. And when we had
had that dinner we went over to it in a launch, all by
ourselves. Wilbur and Miss Lucy and that Miss
Woodbury had to catch a ten o'clock train back to
Tiffin, Ohio, because when you're out with girls like
that you can't get careless and miss any trains and stay
out all night like you can with some kinds of Janes.

And Wilbur blowed himself to the launch and it cost
him fifteen cold plunks, but I wouldn't ever have
knew if I hadn't listened. He wasn't no tin horn
kind of a sport.

Over at the Cedar Point place we didn't stay around
where there was a gang of common kind of cattle
at all.

There was big dance halls and dining places for
yaps, and there was a beach you could walk along and
get where it was dark, and we went there.

She didn't talk hardly at all and neither did I, and I was thinking how glad I was my mother was all right, and always made us kids learn to eat with a fork at table and not swill soup and not be noisy and rough like a gang you see around a race track that way.

Then Wilbur and his girl went away up the beach and Lucy and I set down in a dark place where there was some roots of old trees the water had washed up, and after that, the time, till we had to go back in the launch and they had to catch their trains, wasn't nothing at all. It went like winking your eye.

Here's how it was. The place we were setting in was dark, like I said, and there was the roots from that old stump sticking up like arms, and there was a watery smell, and the night was like—as if you could put your hand out and feel it—so warm and soft and dark and sweet like a orange.

I most cried and I most swore and I most jumped up and danced, I was so mad and happy and sad.

When Wilbur come back from being alone with his girl, and she saw him coming, Lucy she says, "we got to go to the train now," and he was most crying, too, but she never knew nothing I knew, and she couldn't be so all busted up. And then, before Wilbur and Miss Woodbury got up to where she was, she put her face up and kissed me quick and put her head up against me and she was all quivering and—Gee whizz.

Sometime I hope I have cancer and die. I guess you know what I mean. We went in the launch across the bay to the train like that, and it was dark too. She whispered and said it was like she and I could get out of the boat and walk on the water, and it sounded foolish, but I knew what she meant.

And then quick, we were right at the depot, and
there was a big gang of yaps, the kind that goes to the
fairs, and crowded and milling around like cattle, and
how could I tell her? "It won't be long because you'll
write and I'll write to you." That's all she said.

I got a chance like a hay barn afire. A swell chance
I got.

And maybe she would write me, down at Marietta
that way, and the letter would come back, and stamped
on the front of it by the U.S.A. "there ain't any such
guy," or something like that, whatever they stamp
on a letter that way.

And me trying to pass myself off for a bigbug and
a swell—to her, as decent a little body as God ever
made. Craps amighty. A swell chance I got.

And then the train come in and she got on, and
Wilbur Wessen come and shook hands with me and
that Miss Woodbury was nice and bowed to me and I
at her and the train went and I busted out and cried
like a kid.

Gee, I could have run after that train and made Dan
Patch look like a freight train after a wreck, but
socks amighty, what was the use? Did you ever see
such a fool?

I'll bet you what—if I had an arm broke right now
or a train had run over my foot—I wouldn't go to no
doctor at all. I'd go set down and let her hurt and
hurt—that's what I'd do.

I'll bet you what—if I hadn't a drunk that booze
I'd a never been such a boob as to go tell such a lie—
that couldn't never be made straight to a lady like her.

I wish I had that fellow right here that had on a
Windsor tie and carried a cane. I'd smash him for

fair. Gosh darn his eyes. He's a big fool—that's what he is.

And if I'm not another you just go find me one and I'll quit working and be a bum and give him my job. I don't care nothing for working and earning money and saving it for no such boob as myself.

LOVE AND BREAD

By August Strindberg

When young Gustaf Falk, the assistant councilor, made his ceremonial proposal for Louise's hand to her father, the old gentleman's first question was: "How much are you earning?"

"No more than a hundred kroner a month. But Louise—"

"Never mind the rest," interrupted Falk's prospective father-in-law; "you don't earn enough."

"Oh, but Louise and I love each other so dearly! We are so sure of one another."

"Very likely. However, let me ask you: is twelve hundred a year the sum total of your resources?"

"We first became acquainted at Lidingo."

"Do you make anything besides your government salary?" persisted Louise's parent.

"Well, yes, I think we shall have sufficient. And then, you see, our mutual affection—"

"Yes, exactly; but let's have a few figures."

"Oh," said the enthusiastic suitor, "I can get enough by doing extra work!"

"What sort of work? And how much?"

"I can give lessons in French, and also translate. And then I can get some proofreading."

"How much translation?" queried the elder, pencil in hand.

"I can't say exactly, but at present I am translating a French book at the rate of ten kroner per folio."

"How many folios are there altogether?"

"About a couple of dozen, I should say."

"Very well. Put this at two hundred and fifty kroner. Now, how much else?"

"Oh, I don't know. It's a little uncertain."

"What, you are not certain, and you intend to marry? You seem to have queer notions of marriage, young man! Do you realize that there will be children, and that you will have to feed and clothe them, and bring them up?"

"But," objected Falk, "the children may not come so very soon. And we love each other so dearly, that—"

"That the arrival of children may be prophesied quite safely." Then, relenting, Louise's father went on:

"I suppose you are both set on marrying, and I don't doubt but what you are really fond of each other. So it seems as tho I should have to give my consent after all. Only make good use of the time that you are engaged to Louise by trying to increase your income."

Young Falk flushed with joy at this sanction, and demonstratively kissed the old man's hand. Heavens, how happy he was—and his Louise, too! How proud they felt the first time they went out walking together arm in arm, and how everybody noticed the radiant happiness of the engaged couple!

In the evenings he came to see her, bringing with him the proof-sheets he had undertaken to correct. This made a good impression on papa and earned the industrious young man a kiss from his betrothed. But one evening they went to the theater for a change, and

drove home in a cab, the cost of that evening's entertainment amounting to ten kroner. Then, on a few
other evenings, instead of giving the lessons, he called
at the young lady's house to take her for a little walk.

As the day set for the wedding drew near, they had
to think about making the necessary purchases to
furnish their flat. They bought two handsome beds of
real walnut, with substantial spring mattresses and
soft eiderdown quilts. Louise must have a blue quilt,
as her hair was blond. They, of course, also paid a
visit to the house-furnishers', where they selected a
lamp with a red shade, a pretty porcelain statuet
of Venus, a complete table service with knives, forks,
and fine glassware. In picking out the kitchen utensils
they were benefited by mama's advice and aid. It
was a busy time for the assistant councilor—rushing
about to find a house, looking after the workmen,
seeing that all the furniture was got together, writing
out checks, and what not.

Meanwhile it was perfectly natural that Gustaf could
earn nothing extra. But when they were once married
he would easily make it up. They intended to be most
economical—only a couple of rooms to start with.
Anyhow, you could furnish a small apartment better
than a large one. So they took a first-floor apartment at six hundred kroner, consisting of two rooms,
kitchen, and larder. At first Louise said she would
prefer three rooms on the top landing. But what did
it matter, after all, so long as they sincerely loved each
other?

At last the rooms were furnished. The sleeping
chamber was like a small sanctuary, the beds standing
side by side like chariots taking their course along
life's journey. The blue quilts, the snowy sheets, and

the pillow-spreads embroidered with the young people's initials amorously interwined, all had a bright and cheerful appearance. There was a tall, elegant screen for the use of Louise, whose piano—costing twelve hundred kroner—stood in the other chamber, which served as sitting-room, dining-room, and study, in one. Here, too, stood a large walnut writing-desk and dining-table, with chairs to match; a large gilt-framed mirror, a sofa, and a bookcase added to the general air of comfort and coziness.

The marriage ceremony took place on a Saturday night, and late on Sunday morning the happy young couple were still asleep. Gustaf rose first. Altho the bright light of day was peering in through the shutters, he did not open them, but lit the red-shaded lamp, which threw a mysterious rose glow over the porcelain Venus. The pretty young wife lay there languid and content; she had slept well, and had not been awakened—as it was Sunday—by the rumbling of early market wagons. Now the church bells were ringing joyfully, as if to celebrate the creation of man and woman.

Louise turned over, while Gustaf retired behind the screen to put on a few things. He went out into the kitchen to order lunch. How dazzlingly the new copper and tin utensils gleamed and glistened! And all was his own—his and hers. He told the cook to go to the neighboring restaurant, and request that the lunch be sent in. The proprietor knew about it; he had received full instructions the day before. All he needed now was a reminder that the moment had come.

The bridgegroom thereupon returns to the bedchamber and taps softly: "May I come in?"

A little scream is heard. Then: "No, dearest; just wait a minute!"

Gustaf lays the table himself. By the time the lunch arrives from the restaurant, the new plates and cutlery and glasses are set out on the fresh, white linen cloth. The bridal bouquet lies beside Louise's place. As she enters the room in her embroidered morning wrapper, she is greeted by the sunbeams. She still feels a little tired, so he makes her take an arm-chair, and wheels it to the table. A drop or two of liqueur enlivens her; a mouthful of caviar stimulates her appetite. Fancy what mama would say if she saw her daughter drinking spirits! But that's the advantage of being married, you know; then you can do whatever you please.

The young husband waits most attentively upon his fair bride. What a pleasure, too! Of course he has had good luncheons before, in his bachelor days; but what comfort or satisfaction had he ever derived from them? None. Thus he reflects while consuming a plate of oysters and a glass of beer. What numb-skulls they are, those bachelors, not to marry! And how selfish! Why, there ought to be a tax on them, as on dogs. Louise is not quite so severe, urging gently and sweetly that perhaps the poor fellows who elect the single state are subjects of pity. No doubt if they could afford to marry, they would—she thinks. Gustaf feels a slight pang at his heart. Surely happiness is not to be measured by money. No, no; but, but— Well, never mind, there will soon be lots of work, and then everything will run smoothly. For the present there is this delicious roast partridge with cranberry sauce to be considered, and the Burgundy. These luxuries together with some fine artichokes, cause the

young wife a moment's alarm, and she timidly asks
Gustaf if they can afford living on such a scale. But
Gustaf pours more wine into the glass of his little
Louise, reasurring her and softening those groundless
fears. "One day is not every day," he says; "and people ought to enjoy life when they can. Ah, how beautiful life is!"

At six o'clock an elegant carriage, with two horses,
pulls up before the door, and the bridal pair take a
drive. Louise is charmed as they roll along through
the park, reclining there so comfortably, while they
meet acquaintances on foot, who bow to them in obvious astonishment and envy. The assistant councilor
has made a good match, they must think; he has
chosen a girl with money. And they, poor souls, have
to walk. How much pleasanter to ride, without effort,
leaning against these soft cushions! It is symbolical of
agreeable married life.

The first month was one of unceasing enjoyment—
balls, parties, dinners, suppers, theaters. Still, the
time they spent at home was really the best of all! It
was a delightful sensation to carry Louise off home,
from her parents, at night, when they would do as
they pleased under their own roof. Arriving at the
flat, they would make a little supper, and then they
would sit comfortably, chatting until a late hour
Gustaf was all for economy—the theory of it, that is
to say. One day the young bride and housekeeper
tried smoked salmon with boiled potatoes. How she
relished it, too! But Gustaf demurred, and when
smoked salmon day came round again he invested in a
brace of partridges. These he bought at the market
for a krone, exulting over the splendid bargain, of
which Louise did not approve. She had once bought

a pair for less money. Besides, to eat game was ex-
travagant. However, it would not do to disagree with
her husband about such a trifling matter.

After a couple of months more Louise Falk became
strangely indisposed. Had she caught cold? Or had
she perchance been poisoned by the metal kitchen
utensils? The doctor who was called in merely laughed,
and said it was all right—a queer diagnosis, to be sure,
when the young lady was seriously ailing. Perhaps
there was arsenic in the wall-paper. Falk took some
to a chemist, bidding him make a careful analysis.
The chemist's report stated the wall-paper to be quite
free from any harmful substance.

His wife's sickness not abating, Gustaf began to
investigate on his own account, his studies in a medical book resulting in a certainty as to her ailment.
She took warm foot-baths, and in a month's time her
state was declared entirely promising. This was sudden—sooner than they had expected; yet how lovely to
be papa and mama! Of course the child would be
a boy—no doubt of that; and one must think of a name
to give him. Meanwhile, tho, Louise took her husband aside, and reminded him that since their marriage he had earned nothing to supplement his salary,
which had proved far from sufficient. Well, it was
true they had lived rather high, but now a change
should be made, and everything would be satisfactory!

Next day the assistant councilor went to see his
good friend the barrister, with a request that he in-
dorse a promissory note. This would allow him to
borrow the money that would be needed to meet certain unavoidable forthcoming expenses—as Falk made
clear to his friend. "Yes," agreed the man of law.

"marrying and raising a family is an expensive business.
I have never been able to afford it."

Falk felt too much ashamed to press his request, and
when he returned home, empty-handed, was greeted
with the news that two strangers had been to the house,
and had asked for him. They must be lieutenants in
the army, thought Gustaf, friends belonging to the
garrison of Fort Vaxholm. No, he was told, they could
not have been lieutenants; they were much older-look-
ing men. Ah, then they were two fellows he used to
know in Upsala; they had probably heard of his marriage, and had come to look him up. Only the servant
said they were not from Upsala, but were Stock-
holmers, and carried sticks. Mysterious—very; but
no doubt they would come back.

Then the young husband went marketing again. He
bought strawberries—at a bargain, of course.

"Just fancy," he triumphantly exclaimed to his
housewife, "a pint of these large strawberries for a
krone and a half, at this time of year!"

"Oh, but Gustaf dear, we can't afford that sort of
thing!"

"Never mind, darling; I have arranged for some
extra work."

"But what about our debts?"

"Debts? Why, I'm going to make a big loan, and
pay them all off at once that way."

"Ah," declared Louise, "but won't this simply mean
a new debt?"

"No matter if it does. It will be a respite, you
know. But why discuss such unpleasant things? What
capital strawberries, eh, dear? And don't you think a
glass of sherry would go well now after the strawberries?"

Upon which the servant was sent out for a bottle of sherry—the best, naturally.

When Falk's wife awoke from her afternoon nap on the sofa that day, she apologetically reverted to the subject of debt. She hoped he would not be angry at what she had to say. Angry? No, of course not. What was it? Did she want some money for the house? Louise explained:

"The grocer has not been paid, the butcher has threatened us, and the livery-stable man also insists on having his bill settled."

"Is that all?" replied the assistant councilor. "They shall be paid at once—to-morrow—every farthing. But let's think of something else. How would you like to go out for a little drive in the park? You'd rather not take a carriage? All right, then, there's the tramway; that will take us to the park."

So they went to the park, and they had dinner in a private room at the Alhambra Restaurant. It was great fun, too, because the people in the general dining-room thought they were a frisky young pair of lovers. This idea amused Gustaf, tho Louise seemed a trifle depressed, especially when she saw the bill. They could have had a good deal at home for that amount.

The months go by, and now arises the need for actual preparation—a cradle, infant's clothing, and so forth.

Falk has no easy time raising the money. The livery-stable man and the grocer refuse further credit, 'for they, too, have families to feed. What shocking materialism!

At length the eventful day arrives. Gustaf must secure a nurse, and even while holding his new-born daughter in his arms is called out to pacify his creditors. The fresh responsibilities weigh heavily upon him; he almost breaks down under the strain. He succeeds, it is true, in getting some translation to do, but how can he perform the work when at every touch and turn he is obliged to run errands? In this frame of mind he appeals to his father-in-law for help. The old gentleman receives him coldly:

"I will help you this once, but not again. I have little enough myself, and you are not my only child."

Delicacies must be provided for the mother, chicken and expensive wine. And the nurse has to be paid.

Fortunately, Falk's wife is soon on her feet again. She is like a girl once more, with a slender figure. Her pallor is quite becoming. Louise's father talks seriously to his son-in-law, however:

"Now, no more children, if you please, unless you want to be ruined."

For a brief space the junior Falk family continued to live on love and increasing debts. But one day bankruptcy knocked at the door. The seizure of the household effects was threatened. Then the old man came and took Louise and her child, and as they rode off in a cab he made the bitter reflection that he had lent his girl to a young man, who had given her back after a year, dishonored. Louise would willingly have stayed with Gustaf, but there was nothing more to subsist upon. He remained behind, looking on while the bailiffs—those men with the sticks—denuded the flat of everything, furniture, bedding, crockery, cutlery, kitchen utensils, until it was stripped bare.

Now began real life for Gustaf. He managed to get a position as proofreader on a newspaper which was published in the morning, so that he had to work

at his desk for several hours each night. As he had not
actually been declared a bankrupt, he was allowed to
keep his place in the government service, altho he
could hope for no more promotion. His father-in-law
made the concession of letting him see his wife and
child on Sundays, but he was never permitted to be
alone with them. When he left, in the evening, to go
to the newspaper office, they would accompany him to
the gate, and he would depart in utter humiliation of
soul. It might take him perhaps twenty years to pay
off all his obligations. And then—yes, what then?
Could he then support his wife and child? No, probably not. If, in the meantime, his father-in-law should
die, they would be left without a home. So he must
be thankful even to the hard-hearted old man who had
so cruelly separated them.

Ah, yes, human life itself is indeed hard and cruel!
The beasts of the field find maintenance easily enough,
while of all created beings man alone must toil and
spin. It is a shame, yes, it is a crying shame, that in
this life everybody is not provided with gratuitous
partridges and strawberries.

DOWN BAYOU DUBAC

By BARRY BENEFIELD

I reckon I'll never get entirely through answering questions about that Deeves-Mendoza affair, tho my conscience is clear and calm. I was of course in bed that midnight when Ed Deeves tapped at my window. Crebillon is a little town, and bedtime here is nine o'clock for children and grown-ups. Youth is about its own thrilling business from eight until any time at all. It was late May, and in Louisiana it is already good summer then. My wire screens were in place, my bedroom windows wide open. I had not been down Bayou Dubac since the summer before, and I was wondering when I'd get a good chance to go again. Of course I was already fishing a bit in Dubac up here near town, below the railroad tank, but there is nothing this far up except catfish, little perch, and those devilish terrapins that eat your bait and snag your line on a stump. But down the bayou! Lord save us, it's a debauch. If you have a fisherman's passions.

Well, there I was respectably in bed only day-dreaming about real fishing and never expecting any good chance until June, July, and August when the parties of young people would be going down Dubac for four-day picnics and of course taking me along as the chaperon.

The white moon had come up, and I was lying there staring out at the big pine-tree across the street in Mr. Pelletier's back yard, and it looking like a great purple plume set against a silver screen. The wind was cutting up a bit, washing waves of moist air in over me, wind that had but lately kissed a million blooming magnolias. The old clock on the mantel had slowly pounded twelve times on its throbbing coil of wire. Outside the katydids were swinging their tense monotonous rhythm back and forth, back and forth, when suddenly I heard a tapping on my window-sill.

"Who is that?" I called; which was a foolish question, because I was in the shadow, he was in the moonnight, and I could see Ed Deeves' square head, even the color of his brown eyes, as plain as day.

"It's me—Ed Deeves. Mis' Lyd, come on, let's go fishin'."

"To-morrow, Ed?"

"Nome, right now. Could you be down at the wharf by two o'clock, Mis' Lyd? We'll be down Dubac several days anyhow. I'll go get the boat ready an' the supplies in."

It was a short enough trip from my house down to the wharf, goodness knows, and I was afraid he might change his mind if I tried to postpone anything. More than once a fine trip with a strong and willing boy who can pull a boat and cut fire-wood and get fish-bait has been lost to me through postponement, tho seldom do I do the postponing.

"All right, Ed. I'll be there. You wait for me."

"If you don't see me right away when you get there, Mis' Lyd, just whistle like a whippoorwill."

I might have known some mischief was in the air when he said that. When a Southern boy makes a rendezvous and tells somebody to whistle like a whip-poorwill he is up to devilment, or thinks he is. "No, Ed, I will not whistle like that weepy bird, because I can't, but if I fail to find you I'll raise my voice to high heaven."

I travel light through this vale of tears because I never know when I might get a good chance to go down the bayou for a few days I have no cats, chickens, birds, or flowers except some hardy things that can get along by themselves in a pinch. By 1:30 I was footing it through a back street to Crebillon's broken-down old wharf. The infernal railroads killed off our steamboats and well nigh killed poor Crebillon; it's like a little old dried-up man wearing a suit made for him when he was fat and forty. We've enough brick buildings here for a city of thirty thousand—and we have three, no more. And the wharf's going to pieces.

It was easy enough to find that Deeves boy. I just walked along by the old black piles until I heard a low buzzing of talk. "Hallo!" I shouted. Strangely enough I heard the cautious call of a whippoorwill. Ed was already in the boat, and he maneuvered the stern of it around so that I could step in. I am a plump person, but I am *not* a mountain of flesh, and I can handle myself in a boat without a lot of fuss and nonsense. I laid my poles in place, stowed my luggage with Ed's, and felt for the rudder-cords.

"Let's go, Ed," I said briskly. "Who's your friend up there in the seat ahead of you?"

"It's me, Mis' Lyd. I was just waitin' to see if you would recognize me when we got out of the shadow into the middle of the bayou where the moon is."

"Ruth Mendoza! Who'd have thought it—you and Ed Deeves together."

"I've got something to tell you, Mis' Lyd, when we get down to Ed's secret campin' place."

"All right, Ruth; I'll wait. Don't tell me now; I've got to pay strict attention to this rudder. Let's go, Ed." At times there is such a thing as knowing too much. I already knew, as did everybody in town, that after having been Ruth's standard escort since her pigtail days to all the many juvenile gaieties of jolly little Crebillon, Ed had been deliberately frozen out of the Mendoza home. Not that it had been much trouble to freeze Ed out: the Deeveses and all their connections have pride and to spare, especially Ed's mother, who was Fanny Crandall and went to school with me. We all had thought the reason was the Mendoza money, he being a banker, and the Deeves's comparative lack of it, Sam Deeves being a merchant who will give credit to anybody and was never known to foreclose a mortgage on a farmer in his life. And now here were Ed and Ruth going off down the bayou on a grand shylark. No, I did not want to hear too much; I wanted nothing to interfere with this trip down Bayou Dubac.

Well, Ed got his oars in place and laid down to his job. He was then only nineteen and an inch or so short of six feet. When he's forty-five he'll be fat; I know because I was like him. But, saints alive, he was a boy. His sleeves were rolled above his elbows, his thick unstanding tangled sandy hair was uncovered; and his soft-collared shirt wide open in front. The sharp prow of the boat was hissing through the water. He was feathering his oars on the back stroke, but that decorative stuff was for Ruth's benefit; I said nothing.

he'd soon stop that. A heavy lot of luggage, one solid young man, and one entirely ample old widow-woman, not counting a seventeen-year-old 120-pounder, were load enough to discourage any fancy feather-edging on the surface of the water with the oars, which should come clean and clear.

Pretty soon he stopped that foolishness and got down to business. For four hours he pulled steadily on, and when the sun was pinking the east, the pale spent moon being still with us, we turned into the wide mouth of a slough that branched off from the bayou and ran back a mile or so into the deep dark-green woods. Ed pointed to a spot in what seemed to be the shore of the slough where the low-hanging limbs of some sweet-gum trees were dabbling their dainty fingers in the clear water. "Steer to that place, Mis' Lyd," he said. And when we got there, which I thought was the bank behind the limbs, he lifted them and pulled the boat past a lot of trees neck-deep in the slough, and we were out in a small lagoon that nobody could see from the big one when the leaves were on the trees.

At the far end of it the bank rose a hundred feet to level ground, on which were those miraculous tall yellow-pine trees that shoot away up into the air without putting out a limb and then suddenly spread out until their tops touch each other.

"A spring's on the other side of the hill," Ed announced.

"No one ever *could* find us here," breathed Ruth, clasping her hands and looking around with a wicked gleam in her eyes.

"Some fishermen and hunters know it, but not many town people, I reckon. This is where I was goin' to build my log cabin, Mis' Lyd, when I was about to adopt the profession of fishin'." Ed grinned as at the folly of silly youth long past; it had been about three years since he was in that fix.

Within thirty minutes that admirable boy had our skiff up on the hill under the pines, which would keep us dry unless there was a deluge. While Ed was making a fire, and we women were sitting against a copper-colored pine-hole as big around as a hogshead, Ruth leaned over and said, "Mis' Lyd, I want to tell you—"

"No, no, not now, child; I've got to get the things ready to cook; I'll bet that boy is famished, and I know I am. You get the bucket and bring some water from the spring."

I scrambled to my feet and began pottering around in the grub-box. I was afraid she might—I say it may be that I was afraid she might—tell something that would make it necessary to demand that Ed take us right back to town. I knew he would if I told him to; he's that kind of a boy.

Here we were, a boy and a girl and the standard outdoor chaperon of Crebillon; all very proper indeed; and the weather and the water looked prime for fishing, and I hadn't had a good round with real fish since the year before. It hadn't rained in two weeks, so the fish should be hungry. The mist was curling up from the slough like incense. Red birds flashed among the dark-green bushes down near the water, their voices as clear and liquid as it was. The old pines away up there above us were whispering, "Hush, hush, hush!" No, it is possible that I did not want that handsome minx to do any inconvenient confessing.

If loss of appetite is a certain symptom of being, as they say, in love, then that Deeves boy and Ruth

Mendoza were as cold to each other as if they had been hostile neighbors all their lives.

"If this keeps up," Ed moaned, "we'll be out of baker's bread in two days an' have to cook cornbread or biscuit for every meal."

"That's all right, boy," I spoke up comfortingly; "you eat on; we'll want a change of bread, anyway, in two days, and Old Lady Pilduff will cook it. But whatever happens, we can't run out of meat because I feel the fish down there all lined up ready to be mine."

"This place was just waitin' for us," said Ruth in a rapturous whisper. "We'll remember this place an' this time as long as we live, won't we, Ed?" And leaping to her feet, she gave me a prodigious hug, which was of course meant for that big scalawag who was still eating.

"Go on, you two," I said, "and take a walk, while I do the dishes. And, Ed, you look for a dead pine-tree with sawyer grobus under the bark. Don't you dare bring back those brown dried-up ones; get fat white ones that a fish with some pride can eat."

They went away into the woods holding hands and swinging them up and down and touching their shoulders, elbows, and hips as they walked. The place was full of that pair.

Well, it was gorgeous that day, the fishing. We pulled out into the larger slough, Ed knew the sunken tree-tops that were the picnic-grounds of white perch, and I had such an orgy of delight as I had never had before or ever expected to have. A nibble at the hook deep down in the water, a little running, a sweep heavy weight on the line coming nearer and nearer the top—and then smack into the boat. White and black striped

As I say, everybody knew that Ed had been politely shooed away from the Mendoza home, but no one except him and Ruth remembered the time, when he was fifteen, that he had, during one of many and varied ambitious moments, decided to be a telegraph operator and had run a wire from h' bedroom across his father's garden and on across an alley to the tall Mendoza stable that sits away back from the big house. After the freezing out, it now developed, Ruth would go often to the loft at night, give the old telegraph-key a click or two that let him know she was there and the way was clear.

They had reconciled themselves to the plan of Ruth's going away for four years, altho of course she was always to wait for him and never marry the most fascinating New Yorker; and as for Ed, he was to put in ten years making himself a doctor—four years academic, four years medical, two years in a hospital. Ten years, mind you! Yes, they had agreed on that heroic schedule, bless their strong and gallant hearts; but before entering upon it they had planned to meet every night in the Mendoza stable, which was to be a sort of feast to fortify them for the desolate time ahead.

And then the night that Ed tapped at my window, after Ruth had slipped back into her room, she had heard her parents talking and so had discovered that steps had been taken to rush her away at once; whereupon she had gone again to the loft, summoned Ed, and they had cooked up the plan to steal away down the bayou, she leaving a note saying they had run away to New Orleans on the train. Ed, who clerked in his father's store, had a key to it and got supplies and his camping outfit without having to answer ques-

tions. As for my presence, it was due to a thought
of his; a large sop to respectability.

"Just think, Ed, if we hadn't done this I'd be on
the train a hundred miles away from you this very
minute. It takes so little to make us happy, doesn't
it—just to be together? Nobody ought to begrudge
us that." I heard Ruth, with her head lying in the
hollow of his shoulder as if it were made to hold her
head and nothing else, murmuring that. "When you
are away from me, Ed, I feel an ache—no, not like
that exactly: it's as if I were terribly hungry an'
thirsty an' weak, an' when you come it's as if I'd had
food an' drink an' was whole an' strong again. My
blood sings when you're near me, Ed. Do you ever
feel like that?"

"Yes, Ruth, an' you make me feel like a string band
does an' it on a boat going down the bayou almost out
of hearin', an' like rain on the roof when it's hot
weather an' the night is all dark outside, an' like
moonlight on the water, an' flowers on the wind, an'
like I used to feel a long time ago in Sunday-school
when I sang hymns an' the organ played an' all the
other voices caught me an' lifted me up an' up—oh,
Ruth, if you marry a Spanish Jew up there, or anybody at all but me, I don't know what I'll do. I'll be
ruined, I know I will."

Lord save us, I had never known that big bulk of a
boy could talk like that. I'd known he had sense—
Fanny Crandall's son would have—but I'd had an idea
he was dumb at talking.

Well, I lay there, invisible under my mosquito-bar,
listening to the wind whispering away up among the
pine-tops and hoping that nothing would smash the
plans of that perfect pair sitting behind the yellow

flames of the camp-fire. But ten years! Great Cæsar, what a gallant and dangerous schedule! Ed would be a doctor all right if he set out to be, even if he did partly have to work his way through college, but ten years is a *long* time to youth. Loose-mouthed old sinner tho I am, I said in my mind, "Please, God, give that boy his sweetheart, and be quick about it."

The next morning we lay late; it was so cool and dim under the pines that the sun did not wake us, so it was eight o'clock when a raging hunger dragged us to our feet. Again that boy and girl ate like cannibals after a ten-day fast, and Lydia Pilduff was not far behind, if any. Ed didn't much want to go out fishing again in the big slough; he said we had enough fish to do us for two days. But I bedeviled him so that he pulled out to sunken tree-tops that we had not visited the day before. Our luck holding, I was again drunk with the black and white beauties we hauled into the boat. If Ed opened his mouth to speak to Ruth I glowered at him. Fish fly from conversation.

After a while Ed said he was tired of fishing, in which sentiment he was strangely joined by Ruth, and would I mind if he put himself and her ashore, so that they could walk over to the bayou and get some boards from an old half-sunk house-boat with which to build a table for the camp? From motives partly of mercy and partly of self-interest, I agreed to his proposal, paddling back to my watery hunting-grounds after they had set out for Dubac. At our midday dinner they told me that Pink Beddo, a negro fisherman on the way up to town with a load of fish, had seen them working on the house-boat.

In the afternoon I paddled out to catch still more

fish, leaving that blessed pair alone to piddle around building their table and to be together. Their precious moments were slipping away fast. At the most they had but a few days, and their Eden might come to an end at any time now.

That night, lying on my pine-straw, I heard them once more talking over by the fire, their backs against their favorite log.

"That fisherman will give us away, Ed; yes, he will, I just know it. There will be such a hullabaloo in town about us that he will hear of it, and he will then say he saw us down here. Ed, I want you to take a long look at me, so when you come back an' meet me on the street you'll know who I am. Ten years! You'll be twenty-nine an' I'll be twenty-seven. Then you won't look at me unless I pretend to be sick an' send for you, an' then you'll just look at my *tongue!* Look at me now, Ed, an' tell me what you see."

"I see black hair—"

"Oh, fine; he knows my hair is black."

"I see black hair that lies against a forehead as white an' smooth as marble."

"And as solid, honey?"

"All right, I won't say any more."

He searched with much ado through four or five pockets, found his pipe, knocked it and scraped it and filled it; and Ruth waiting patiently with her head down, looking at him no doubt out of the corner of her eye, until his pipe was thoroughly lit.

"Now, Ed, go on; tell me some more."

He made no answer, but sat staring out across the slough, where the little waves were running after the white moon.

"Ed, we won't have each other long down here, will we? An' now you're mad at me."

"And your eyes, Ruth, are like deep black pools, but away down in them are little bonfires that beckon at me. Sometimes when you are quiet your eyes look so sad it's like a stab to me; your father's are like that too. But then they dance when you are happy. And there's your jolly straight little nose, like a Greek's in my history-book, that runs so much further up between your eyes than mine does. And there's your mouth that crinkles at the corners; I think smiles hide there so they can come out quick. And your impudent proud chin that says, 'I'm not afraid of anybody.' An' I'll remember your face always so tense as if you were forever *terribly* interested in something; an' your walk, swaggerin' like a boy an' takin' *enormous* steps for a girl of five-foot-three. All mine, mine; an' if when I'm ready to support you Mr. Mendoza will not give you to me, then I'll take you, an' it'll make no difference where you are, either—Crebillon, New York, anywhere."

"Oh, pull me tight against you, Ed, an' kiss me a thousand times. Oh, there, there, no more; I'm a little drunk, I think, with them. But all the stars that ever were are singing inside of me, an' I can feel that the world really is only a little ball flyin' round, with me on the very edge of it almost fallin' off. Be still, honey, an' hold me just this way, an' let's hear what the night is sayin'."

"I hear your heart beatin', Ruth."

"I hear the woods breathin', Ed."

"I hear a sleepy bird singin', Ruth, away over yonder by the bayou, like he was afraid he would go to sleep before he finished his song."

"I hear the pines talkin' in little voices away up there above us."

"Listen, Ruth, there's somethin' small an' afraid stealin' about in the leaves over there among the buckeye bushes; maybe it's a red fox-squirrel, or a little molly cottontail rabbit, or maybe an old mother possum with four babies sittin' on her back an' holdin' to her tail."

"Be quiet, Ed; you might scare her, bless her old heart. Oh, honey, on such a night as this, with you against my heart, I love everything that is on this earth. I reckon, on such a night as this is, a thousand, thousand other people are lovin' each other, but no two of them are so happy as we, Ed, are they?"

"No, Ruth."

After a deep round-eyed silence she went on: "Ed, wouldn't it just be fine if we could go to college *together?* We'd board the first four years, because I'd be as busy as you with classes; but later while you were in the medical school and in the hospital I'd keep house, and every night you could come back *home* even if it were only two rooms an' a kitchen. Oh, I know what you are thinkin', that maybe I'd have a baby before I got out of college. Well, if I did I'd quit school in a minute. One baby could teach me more, more that I want to know anyway, than ten professors could in a year; not because he would know more but because I'd pay more attention to what he said."

"Oh, Ruth, you do talk like a glorious fairy-tale! Gee, I could work my head off with you near-by. But it's no use at all goin' on this way. I just naturally can't support you now; Mr. Mendoza will have to do that for ten years yet. My dad never promised to do anything except to help me if I'd help myself with summer jobs an' outside work while in college—and now maybe he won't help me at all. He'll try to beat me up when he first sees me, but he never stays mad long."

"If he won't help you, then I'll be the cause of it, because I put it in your head to come down here. Oh, dear, maybe it would have been better if you'd never known me at all, Ed."

"Don't you worry, Ruth; I'll work it through—and I'll come for you when I'm an M. D. Do you have any faith in me, Ruth?"

"Why, all my faith is in you, Ed. I'd as soon expect the sun to drop straight down out of the sky, like an old black burned-out sky-rocket, as you to fail."

And so they sat still, her head on his shoulder, staring with great eyes into the red heart of the fire. And after a while I felt Ruth's soft body against mine.

The next morning came marching up the eastern sky trailing white banners ten miles long. The air was still, the water smooth, and I saw a third sinful day ahead of me; so much mortal delight must be sinful, I felt. But tho Ed and Ruth went out and got me a huge supply of bait they asked if they could not stay in camp and "tidy things up a bit"; and at eleven o'clock Ed was going to start cooking cornbread, which takes a long time in a baking-skillet. I paddled out into the little slough and set out my lines with trembling hands, not knowing how soon our fishing would be over. When the sun stood straight above me I made camp with thirteen fat brem and a soft-shelled turtle, having a mind for turtle soup that night. Ed was stooping by the fire piling hot coals on top of the baking-skillet, Ruth by his side giving directions. I was out behind a pine-tree washing my hands when I heard rowlocks out in the big slough.

"There they are, drat their hides," I grumbled, suddenly hot and cold as if I were terribly mad. Standing on a stump, I could see two boats headed for the hidden mouth of our little slough, and in the rear boat I recognized black Pink Beddo—confound him, I hate him yet—and fat Mr. Flagger, the Methodist minister, who is a poor preacher but a grand fisherman. Mr. Deeves seemed to be saying something to him, and then the second boat stopped outside, the first one coming on.

I called to Ruth and Ed, who had just woke up to the sound of the rowlocks: "I'm going to disappear. If they come, and they will, don't speak about me until I tell you to. Don't say much of anything if you can help it, especially you, Ed; let *them* do the talking." So saying, I scuttled into a near-by thicket of buckeye bushes and sat down out of sight but within easy hearing distance of the camp-fire.

It was in plain sight of the little slough, and presently I heard a boat-chain rattling as it was pulled up on the bank. Parting the bushes, I looked out: Ed and Ruth had not tried to run, they stood side by side awaiting their visitors. Then I saw Mr. Deeves, who is a fiery little man that takes quick, firm, short steps like a goat, rush up to Ed and draw back his first. But the big boy just looked at him, and nothing happened.

"You've disgraced this girl, yourself, an' your family, you whelp, you. I ought to shoot you, an'

I think I would if I'd had sense enough to bring my gun."

"Never mind, Mr. Deeves," put in Mr. Mendoza, laying a hand on his shoulder. "That wouldn't help anybody, would it? Let's sit down."

He let himself down on the log in front of the fire. Ed, his sunburned face sort of ashy and set, stooped down over his baking-skillet, lifted the top off with a stick, gazed long and solemnly at his bread, saw that it was good and brown, and pulled the skillet off its bed of coals. Then he calmly dumped the coals off the top of the skillet, put it back over the bread, and sat down on the log, six feet away from Mr. Mendoza. Sam Deeves was charging around in a circle—which was a good thing because he was working off a lot of steam that wasn't needed—stamping the earth with his tiny feet and glaring now at Ed and now at Ruth. The little father—Mr. Mendoza was no bigger than Sam—turned his black eyes on Ruth, who had taken her stand behind Ed, her hands on his shoulders.

"Well, Ruth, you've made a mess of it, haven't you?"

Ruth's chin was in the air, and she stared out across the slough and offered no answer to the question put to her.

"Yes," broke in Sam, stopping and pointing a dramatically accusing finger at her, "an' *you've* got to marry. You've both disgraced yourselves, but you've got to do that anyway. Down here together alone for two nights!"

"Three nights," said Ruth calmly.

I had known what was coming when I saw that second boat with the preacher in it. I trembled at the thought of what Ed might do. If he began excusing himself and telling about me he would be playing his cards like a washerwoman. I rattled the bushes around me, and I could see him lift his head.

"Why, Mr. Deeves, we just *couldn't* marry now," said Ruth, her voice sweet and poisonous, but those men didn't notice the poison. Any woman would have suspected something wrong at once. "Ed is goin' to be a doctor, as you know, sir, an' that will take ten years. We'd agreed to wait, an' I was goin' to New York to get ready for school, an' we only ran away because I heard mama and papa sayin' Monday night that they had prepared to send me away the very next day. We'd been meetin', secretly because we had to meet that way, an' we were lookin' forward to seein' each other all through this last week; an' when I heard that we were likely to lose even that if we didn't do something we came off down here so as not to lose it. But we agreed all the time that I should go to New York next Monday, which was the time first set."

"Maybe Mr. Mendoza will not now choose to send you to New York, young lady," Sam shot at her.

"Oh, fine! I was just goin' to please him. I'd rather wait for Ed at home."

"And maybe I'll not choose to help that young pup get through college either."

"He'll make his own way then, Mr. Deeves. Ed wants to be a doctor, an' he's goin' to be. There's no doubt about *that*."

"Is that so?"

"It is, sir; and if you weren't Ed's father I'd—"

"Now, now, Ruth, be still," put in Mr. Mendoza soothingly. "Of course you an' Ed had better marry, an' this afternoon probably. We've got a license, an' Mr. Flagger's out yonder in a boat behind the trees."

"Really, daddy, I don't think I ought to do it now,"

and I saw Ruth dig her fingers into Ed's shoulders. "I couldn't stand to have him go off an' leave me right after marryin' me. I'd rather wait if we couldn't go together."

"Bosh!" snorted Sam. "You don't know what's good for you."

"We've thought of that," went on Mr. Mendoza quietly. "Ruth, we're goin' to put together the money I'd have spent on you within the next ten years and what Mr. Deeves meant to give Ed, and you two can go as far on that as you can; go together if you like; or you, Ruth, may stay at home part or all the time."

She went tearing around the end of the log and flung herself on her father's neck. "Oh, daddy, we'll go together; we'd talked of that, but we thought it wasn't any more possible than a fairy-tale."

And then she flew down to the edge of the water, and I heard her shouting in a voice that was a song, "Mr. Flagger, oh, Mr. Flagger, come on, come on quick."

Well, they did it there in the cathedral quietness and dimness of the pine forest; and when it was done, and they were making a lot of noise, I crawled out of the farther side of the thicket from them, walked out into the woods, circled around, and came sauntering back into camp, humming a merry little housewife's tune. When I hove in sight of the party I shouted: "Hello, hello; we didn't expect visitors. Welcome, friends; you come just in time for dinner, therefore thrice welcome of course. Ed, I couldn't find any fish-bait, so you'll have to look for it yourself after dinner. Let's have a grand feast. Sam, you all bring up all

those nice things I know you brought along. We've got
the fish, a hundred pounds of them."

Before I had come up to the party Ruth ran out
to me and buried her head in my bosom. Tiptoeing,
she whispered in my ear, "Mis' Lyd, you're a wizard.
You've caught me a whale, an' I love every pound
of him an' you too."

"Have you been here all the time?" Sam asked sourly
when I walked in among them and began shaking
hands with Ed, who was dry-grinning like a possum,
as if I'd just heard from Ruth the news. "If we'd
only known you were here—"

Well, that blessed pair decided to stay out their week
in the woods, especially as they wouldn't be going away
to college until the fall. They begged me to remain
with them, but I said, "No, I'm kind of tired of fishing; I'm crazy to get home." As we pulled away from
the camp late that afternoon, leaving behind that
heavenly fishing-place and that miraculously lucky
time, my heart was like to break. "But they fill the
woods themselves," I whispered to myself, "and now
you'd be in their way."

"Next summer we'll do it again, Mis' Lyd, won't
we?" shouted Ruth, waving her hat, her hair full of
flowers. "And *every* summer after this."

I had no voice to shout back at her, but I daintily
fluttered a four-inch handkerchief like a silly old fool.
"Next summer," I moaned in my soul, "I may be
dead; and, anyway, never in a thousand years will the
fish bite like this again for me." And they haven't.

THE DISTRICT DOCTOR

By Ivan Turgenev

One day in autumn on my way back from a remote part of the country I caught cold and fell ill. Fortunately the fever attacked me in the district town at the inn; I sent for the doctor. In half-an-hour the district doctor appeared, a thin, dark-haired man of middle height. He prescribed me the usual sudorific, ordered a mustard-plaster to be put on, very deftly slid a five-ruble note up his sleeve, coughing drily and looking away as he did so, and then was getting up to go home, but somehow fell into talk and remained. I was exhausted with feverishness; I foresaw a sleepless night, and was glad of a little chat with a pleasant companion. Tea was served. My doctor began to converse freely. He was a sensible fellow, and expressed himself with vigor and some humor. Queer things happen in the world: you may live a long while with some people, and be on friendly terms with them, and never once speak openly with them from your soul; with others you have scarcely time to get acquainted, and all at once you are pouring out to him—or he to you—all your secrets, as tho you were at confession. I don't know how I gained the confidence of my new friend—anyway, with nothing to lead up to it, he told me a rather curious incident; and here I will report his tale for the information of the indul-

gent reader. I will try to tell it in the doctor's own
words.

"You don't happen to know," he began in a weak and
quavering voice (the common result of the use of un-
mixed Berezov snuff); "you don't happen to know the
judge here, Mylov, Pavel Lukich? . . . You don't
know him? . . . Well, it's all the same." (He
cleared his throat and rubbed his eyes.) "Well, you
see, the thing happened, to tell you exactly without
mistake, in Lent, at the very time of the thaws. I was
sitting at his house—our judge's, you know—playing
preference. Our judge is a good fellow, and fond of
playing preference. Suddenly" (the doctor made fre-
quent use of this word, suddenly) "they tell me,
'There's a servant asking for you.' I say, 'What does
he want?' They say, 'He has brought a note—it must
be from a patient.' 'Give me the note,' I say. So it
is from a patient—well and good—you understand—
it's our bread and butter. . . . But this is how it
was: a lady, a widow, writes to me; she says, 'My
daughter is dying. Come, for God's sake!' she says,
'and the horses have been sent for you.' . . . Well,
that's all right. But she was twenty miles from the
town, and it was midnight out of doors, and the roads
in such a state, my word! And as she was poor herself, one could not expect more than two silver rubles,
and even that problematic; and perhaps it might only
be a matter of a roll of linen and a sack of oatmeal in
payment. However, duty, you know, before everything: a fellow-creature may be dying. I hand over
my cards at once to Kalliopin, the member of the
provincial commission, and return home. I look; a
wretched little trap was standing at the steps, with
peasant's horses, fat—too fat—and their coat as shaggy

as felt; and the coachman sitting with his cap off out of respect. 'Well,' I think to myself, 'it's clear, my friend, these patients aren't rolling in riches.' . . . You smile; but I tell you, a poor man like me has to take everything into consideration. . . . If the coachman sits like a prince, and doesn't touch his cap, and even sneers at you behind his beard, and flicks his whip—then you may bet on six rubles. But this case, I saw, had a very different air. 'However,' I think, 'there's no help for it; duty before everything.' I snatch up the most necessary drugs, and set off. Will you believe it? I only just managed to get there at all. The road was infernal: streams, snow, water-courses, and the dyke had suddenly burst there—that was the worst of it! However, I arrived at last. It was a little thatched house. There was a light in the windows; that meant they expected me. I was met by an old lady, very venerable, in a cap. 'Save her!' she says; 'she is dying.' I say, 'Pray don't distress yourself—where is the invalid?' 'Come this way.' I see a clean little room, a lamp in the corner; on the bed a girl of twenty, unconscious. She was in a burn-ing heat, and breathing heavily—it was fever. There were two other girls, her sisters, scared and in tears. 'Yesterday,' they tell me, 'she was perfectly well and had a good appetite; this morning she complained of her head, and this evening, suddenly, you see, like this.' I say again: 'Pray don't be uneasy.' It's a doctor's duty, you know—and I went up to her and bled her, told them to put on a mustard-plaster, and prescribed a mixture. Meantime I looked at her; I looked at her, you know—there, by God! I had never seen such a face!—she was a beauty, in a word! I felt quite shaken with pity. Such lovely features; such eyes!

. . . But, thank God she became easier; she fell
into a perspiration, seemed to come to her senses,
looked round, smiled, and passed her hand over her
face. . . . Her sisters bent over her. They ask,
'How are you?' 'All right,' she says, and turns away.
I look at her; she had fallen asleep. 'Well,' I say, 'now
the patient should be left alone.' So we all went out
on tiptoe; only a maid remained, in case she was
wanted. In the parlor there was a samovar standing
on the table, and a bottle of rum; in our profession one
can't get on without it. They gave me tea; asked me
to stop the night. . . . I consented: where could I
go, indeed, at that time of night? The old lady kept
groaning. 'What is it?' I say. 'She will live; don't
worry yourself; you had better take a little rest yourself; it is about two o'clock.' 'But will you send to
wake me if anything happens?' 'Yes, yes.' The old
lady went away, and the girls too went to their own
room; they made up a bed for me in the parlor. Well,
I went to bed—but I could not get to sleep, for a wonder! for in reality I was very tired. I could not get
my patient out of my head. At last I could not put
up with it any longer; I got up suddenly; I think to
myself, 'I will go and see how the patient is getting on.'
Her bedroom was next to the parlor. Well, I got up,
and gently opened the door—how my heart beat! I
looked in: the servant was asleep, her mouth wide open,
and even snoring, the wretch! but the patient lay with
her face towards me, and her arms flung wide apart,
poor girl! I went up to her . . . when suddenly
she opened her eyes and stared at me! 'Who is it?
who is it?' I was in confusion. 'Don't be alarmed,
madam,' I say; 'I am the doctor; I have come to see
how you feel.' 'You the doctor?' 'Yes, the doctor;

your mother sent for me from the town; we have bled you, madam; now pray go to sleep, and in a day or two, please God! we will set you on your feet again.' 'Ah, yes, yes, doctor, don't let me die . . . please, please.' 'Why do you talk like that? God bless you!' She is in a fever again, I think to myself; I felt her pulse; yes, she was feverish. She looked at me, and then took me by the hand. 'I .will tell you why I don't want to die; I will tell you. . . . Now we are alone; and only, please don't you . . . not to any one . . . Listen. . . .' I bent down; she moved her lips quite to my ear; she touched my cheek with her hair—I confess my head went round—and began to whisper. . . . I could make out nothing of it. . . . Ah, she was delirious! . . . She whispered and whispered, but so quickly, and as if it were not in Russian; at last she finished, and shivering dropped her head on the pillow, and threatened me with her finger: 'Remember, doctor, to no one.' I calmed her somehow, gave her something to drink, waked the servant, and went away."

At this point the doctor again took snuff with ex- asperated energy, and for a moment seemed stupefied by its effects.

"However," he continued, "the next day, contrary to my expectations, the patient was no better. I thought and thought, and suddenly decided to remain there, even tho my other patients were expecting me. . . . And you know one can't afford to disre- gard that; one's practise suffers if one does. But, in the first place, the patient was really in danger; and secondly, to tell the truth, I felt strongly drawn to her. Besides, I liked the whole family. Tho they were really badly off, they were singularly, I may say, cultivated people. . . . Their father had been a learned man, an author; he died, of course, in poverty, but he had managed before he died to give his children an excellent education; he left a lot of books too. Either because I looked after the invalid very carefully, or for some other reason, anyway, I can venture to say all the household loved me as if I were one of the family. . . . Meantime the roads were in a worse state than ever; all communications, so to say, were cut off completely; even medicine could with difficulty be got from the town. . . . The sick girl was not getting better. . . . Day after day, and day after day . . . but . . . here. . . ." (The doctor made a brief pause.) "I declare I don't know how to tell you. . . ." (He again took snuff, coughed, and swallowed a little tea.) "I will tell you without beating about the bush. My patient . . . how should I say? . . . Well, she had fallen in love with me . . . or, no, it was not that she was in love . . . however . . . really, how should one say?" (The doctor looked down and grew red.) "No," he went on quickly, "in love, indeed! A man should not over-estimate himself. She was an educated girl, clever and well-read, and I have even forgotten my Latin, one may say, completely. As to appearance" (the doctor looked himself over with a smile), "I am nothing to boast of there either. But God Almighty did not make me a fool; I don't take black for white; I know a thing or two; I could see very clearly, for instance, that Aleksandra Andreyevna—that was her name—did not feel love for me, but had a friendly, so to say, inclination—a respect or something for me. Tho she herself perhaps mistook this sentiment, anyway this was her attitude; you may form your own judgment of it. But," added the doctor, who had brought out all these disconnected sentences without taking breath, and with obvious embarrassment, "I seem to be wandering rather—you won't understand anything like this. . . . There, with your leave, I will relate it all in order."

He drank off a glass of tea, and began in a calmer voice.

"Well, then. My patient kept getting worse. You are not a doctor, my good sir; you cannot understand what passes in a poor fellow's heart, especially at first, when he begins to suspect that the disease is getting the upper hand of him. What becomes of his belief in himself? You suddenly grow so timid; it's indescribable. You fancy then that you have forgotten everything you knew, and that the patient has no faith in you, and that other people begin to notice how distracted you are, and tell you the symptoms with reluctance; that they are looking at you suspiciously, whispering. . . . Ah! its horrid! There must be a remedy, you think, for this disease, if one could find it. Isn't this it? You try—no, that's not it! You don't allow the medicine the necessary time to do good. . . . You clutch at one thing, then at another. Sometimes you take up a book of medical prescriptions—here it is, you think! Sometimes, by Jove, you pick one out by chance, thinking to leave it to fate. . . . But meantime a fellow-creature's dying, and another doctor would have saved him. 'We must have a consultation,' you say; 'I will not take the responsibility on myself.' And what a fool you look at such times! Well, in time you learn to bear it; it's nothing to you. A man has died—but it's not your fault; you treated him by the rules. But what's still more torture to you is to see blind faith in you, and to feel yourself that you are not able to be of use. Well, it was just this blind faith that the whole of Aleksandra Andreyevna's family had in me; they had forgotten to think that their daughter was in danger. I, too, on my side assure them that it's nothing, but meantime my heart sinks into my boots. To add to our troubles, the roads were in such a state that the coachman was gone for whole days together to get medicine. And I never left the patient's room; I could not tear myself away; I tell her amusing stories, you know, and play cards with her. I watch by her side at night. The old mother thanks me with tears in her eyes; but I think to myself, 'I don't deserve your gratitude.' I frankly confess to you—there is no object in concealing it now—I was in love with my patient. And Aleksandra Andreyevna had grown fond of me; she would not sometimes let any one be in her room but me. She began to talk to me, to ask me questions; where I had studied, how I lived, who are my people, whom I go to see. I feel that she ought not to talk; but to forbid her to—to forbid her resolutely, you know—I could not. Sometimes I held my head in my hands, and asked myself, 'What are you doing, villain?' . . . And she would take my hand and hold it, give me a long, long look, and turn away, sigh, and say, 'How good you are!' Her hands were so feverish, her eyes so large and languid. . . . 'Yes,' she says, 'you are a good, kind man; you are not like our neighbors. . . . No, you are not like that. . . . Why did I not know you till now!' 'Aleksandra Andreyevna, calm yourself,' I say. . . . 'I feel, believe me, I don't know how I have gained . . . but there, calm yourself . . . All will be right; you will be well again.' And meanwhile I must tell you," continued the doctor, bending forward and raising his eyebrows, "that they associated very little with the neighbors, because the smaller people were not on their level, and pride hindered them from being friendly with the rich. I tell you, they were an exceptionally cultivated family; so you know it was gratifying for me. She would only take her medicine from my hands . . . she would lift herself up, poor girl, with my aid, take it, and gaze at me. . . . My heart felt as if it were bursting. And meanwhile she was growing worse and worse, worse and worse, all the time; she will die, I think to myself; she must die. Believe me, I would sooner have gone to the grave myself; and here were her mother and sisters watching me, looking into my eyes . . . and their faith in me was wearing away. 'Well? how is she?' 'Oh, all right, all right!' All right, indeed! My mind was failing me. Well, I was sitting one night alone again by my patient. The maid was sitting there too, and snoring away in full swing; I can't find fault with the poor girl, tho, she was worn out too. Aleksandra Andreyevna had felt very unwell all the evening; she was very feverish. Until midnight she kept tossing about; at last she seemed to fall asleep; at least, she lay still without stirring. The lamp was burning in the corner before the holy image. I sat there, you know, with my head bent; I even dozed a little. Suddenly it seemed as tho some one touched me in the side; I turned round. . . . Good God! Aleksandra Andreyevna was gazing with intent eyes at me . . . her lips parted, her cheeks seemed burning. 'What is it?' 'Doctor, shall I die?' 'Merciful Heavens!' 'No, doctor, no; please don't tell me I shall live . . . don't say so. . . . If you knew. . . .

Listen! for God's sake don't conceal my real position,'
and her breath came so fast. 'If I can know for
certain that I must die . . . then I will tell you all—
all!' 'Aleksandra Andreyevna, I beg!' 'Listen; I have
not been asleep at all . . . I have been looking at you
a long while. . . . For God's sake! . . . I believe
in you; you are a good man, an honest man; I entreat
you by all that is sacred in the world—tell me the
truth! If you knew how important it is for me. . . .
Doctor, for God's sake tell me. . . . Am I in danger?'
'What can I tell you, Aleksandra Andreyevna, pray?'
'For God's sake, I beseech you!' 'I can't disguise from
you,' I say, 'Aleksandra Andreyevna; you are certainly
in danger; but God is merciful.' 'I shall die, I shall
die.' And it seemed as tho she were pleased, her
face grew so bright; I was alarmed. 'Don't be afraid,
don't be afraid! I am not frightened of death at all.'
She suddenly sat up and leaned on her elbow. 'Now
. . . yes, now I can tell you that I thank you with
my whole heart . . . that you are kind and good—
that I love you!' I stare at her, like one possessed;
it was terrible for me, you know. 'Do you hear, I
love you!' 'Aleksandra Andreyevna, how have I deserved—' 'No, no, you don't—you don't understand
me.' . . . And suddenly she stretched out her arms,
and taking my head in her hands, she kissed it. . . .
Believe me, I almost screamed aloud. . . . I threw
myself on my knees, and buried my head in the pillow.
She did not speak; her fingers trembled in my hair;
I listen; she is weeping. I began to soothe her, to
assure her. . . . I really don't know what I did say
to her. 'You will wake up the girl,' I say to her;
"Aleksandra Andreyevna, I think you . . . believe me
. . . calm yourself.' 'Enough, enough!' she persisted;

'never mind all of them; let them wake, then; let them
come in—it does not matter; I am dying, you see.
. . . And what do you fear? why are you afraid?
Lift up your head. . . . Or, perhaps, you don't love
me; perhaps I am wrong. . . . In that case, forgive
me.' 'Aleksandra Andreyevna, what are you saying!
. . . I love you, Aleksandra Andreyevna.' She looked
straight into my eyes, and opened her arms wide.
'Then take me in your arms.' I tell you frankly, I
don't know how it was I did not go mad that night.
I feel that my patient is killing herself; I see that she
is not fully herself; I understand, too, that if she did
not consider herself on the point of death, she would
never have thought of me; and, indeed, say what you
will, it's hard to die at twenty without having known
love; this was what was torturing her; this was why,
in despair, she caught at me—do you understand now?
But she held me in her arms, and would not let me
go. 'Have pity on me, Aleksandra Andreyevna, and
have pity n yourself,' I say. 'Why,' she says; 'what
is there to think of? You know I must die. . . .'
This she repeated incessantly. . . . 'If I knew that
I should return to life, and be a proper young lady
again, I should be ashamed . . . of course, ashamed
. . . but why now?' 'But who has said you will die?'
'Oh, no, leave off! you will not deceive me; you don't
know how to lie—look at your face. . . .' 'You
shall live, Aleksandra Andreyevna; I will cure you;
we will ask your mother's blessing . . . we will be
united—we will be happy.' 'No, no, I have your
word; I must die . . . you have promised me . . .
you have told me. . . .' It was cruel for me—cruel
for many reasons. And see what trifling things can do
sometimes; it seems nothing at all, but it's painful. It

occurred to her to ask me, what is my name; not my
surname, but my first name. I must needs be so
unlucky as to be called Trifon. Yes, indeed; Trifon
Ivanich. Every one in the house called me doctor.
However, there's no help for it. I say, 'Trifon,
madam.' She frowned, shook her head, and muttered
something in French—ah, something unpleasant, of
course!—and then she laughed—disagreeably too.
Well, I spent the whole night with her in this way.
Before morning I went away, feeling as tho I were
mad. When I went again into her room it was day-
time, after morning tea. Good God! I could scarcely
recognize her; people are laid in their grave looking
better than that. I swear to you, on my honor, I don't
understand—I absolutely don't understand—now, how
I lived through that experience. Three days and nights
my patient still lingered on. And what nights! What
things she said to me! And on the last night—only
imagine to yourself—I was sitting near her, and kept
praying to God for one thing only: 'Take her,' I said,
'quickly, and me with her.' Suddenly the old mother
comes unexpectedly into the room. I had already the
evening before told her—the mother—there was little
hope, and it would be well to send for a priest. When
the sick girl saw her mother she said: 'It's very well
you have come; look at us, we love one another—we
have given each other our word.' 'What does she say,
doctor? what does she say?' I turned livid. 'She is
wandering,' I say; 'the fever.' But she: 'Hush, hush;
you told me something quite different just now, and
have taken my ring. Why do you pretend? My
mother is good—she will forgive—she will understand—
and I am dying. . . . I have no need to tell lies;
give me your hand.' I jumped up and ran out of the

room. The old lady, of course, guessed how it was.

"I will not, however, weary you any longer, and to me too, of course, it's painful to recall all this. My patient passed away the next day. God rest her soul!" the doctor added, speaking quickly and with a sigh. "Before her death she asked her family to go out and leave me alone with her."

" 'Forgive me,' she said; 'I am perhaps to blame towards you . . . my illness . . . but believe me, I have loved no one more than you . . . do not forget me . . . keep my ring.' "

The doctor turned away; I took his hand.

"Ah!" he said, "let us talk of something else, or would you care to play preference for a small stake? It is not for people like me to give way to exalted emotions. There's only one thing for me to think of; how to keep the children from crying and the wife from scolding. Since then, you know, I have had time to enter into lawful wedlock, as they say. . . . Oh . . . I took a merchant's daughter—seven thousand for her dowry. Her name's Akulina; it goes well with Trifon. She is an ill-tempered woman, I must tell you, but luckily she's asleep all day. . . . Well, shall it be preference?"

We sat down to preference, for halfpenny points. Trifon Ivanich won two rubles and a half from me, and went home late, well pleased with his success.

A NEW YEAR'S EVE CONFESSION

By Hermann Sudermann

Thanks be to God, dear lady, that I may once more sit beside you for a peaceful chat. The holiday tumult is past, and you have a little leisure for me again.

Oh, this Christmas season! I believe that it was invented by some evil demon expressly to annoy us poor bachelors, to show us the more clearly all the desolation of our homeless existence. For others a source of joy, it is for us a torture. Of course, I know, we are not all entirely lonely—for us also the joy of making others happy may blossom, that joy upon which rests the whole secret of the blessed holiday mood. But the pleasure of joining in the happiness of others is tainted for us by a touch of self-irony partly, and also by that bitter longing to which—in contrast to homesickness—, I would give the name of "marriage sickness."

Why didn't I come to pour out my heart to you? you ask, you pitying soul, you—you that can give of your sympathy in the same rich measure that others of your sex save for their dainty malices. There's a reason. You remember what Speidel says in his delightful *Lonely Sparrows*, which you sent me the day after Christmas, with a true perception of my state of mind? "The bachelor by instinct," he says, "does not desire comfort. Once he is unhappy he wishes to have the full enjoyment of his unhappiness."

Besides the "lonely sparrow" whom Speidel portrays, there is another sort of bachelor, the so-called "friend of the family." By this I do not mean those professional wreckers of homes, in whose eyes the serpent glitters as they settle down comfortably at the hospitable hearthstone. I mean the good uncle, papa's former school friend, who rocks the baby on his knee while he reads the magazine essays to mama, carefully omitting all the doubtful portions.

I know men who give up their entire lives to the service of some family whose friendship they have won —men who live on without desire by the side of a beautiful woman whom in their hearts they secretly adore.

You doubt me? Oh, it is the words "without desire" that disturb you? You are right, perhaps. In the depth of even the tamest heart some wild desire lies, but—understand me here—it lies bound in chains.

As an instance I would like to tell you about a conversation which took place day before yesterday, on New Year's Eve, between two old, two very old, gentlemen. It is my secret how I came to know of this conversation, and I ask you not to let it go any further. May I begin, then?

Picture to yourself, as a setting for my story, a high-ceilinged room, old-fashioned in furnishings, lighted by a green-shaded, impertinently bright hanging-lamp of the sort our parents had in use before the era of petroleum. The cone of light that goes out from the flame falls upon a round, white-clothed table, upon which stands the various ingredients for a New-Year's punch, while several drops of oil show out broadly in the center of the table.

My two old gentlemen sat half in the shadow of the green lamp-shade, moldering ruins both, from long-past days, bowed and trembling, gazing before them with the dull glance of the dimming eyes of age. One, the host, is evidently an old officer, as you would recognize at once from his carefully wound cravat, his pointed, sharply cut mustache, and his martial eyebrows. He sits holding the handle of his roller-chair like a crutch tightly clasped in both hands. He is motionless except for his jaws, which move up and down ceaselessly with the motion of chewing. The other, who sits near him on the sofa, a tall, spare figure, his narrow shoulders crowned by the high-domed head of a thinker, draws occasional thin puffs of smoke from a long pipe which is just about to go out. Among the myriad wrinkles of his smooth-shaven, dried-up face, framed in a wreath of snow-white curls, there lurked a quiet, gentle smile, a smile which the peace of resignation alone can bring to the face of age.

The two were silent. In the perfect stillness of the room the soft bubbling of the burning oil mingled with the soft bubbling of the tobacco juice. Then, from the darkness of the background, the hanging clock began to announce hoarsely the eleventh hour. "This is the hour when she would begin to make the punch," said the man with the domed forehead. His voice was soft, with a slight vibration.

"Yes, this is the time," repeated the other. The sound of his speech was hard, as if the rattle of command still lingered in it.

"I did not think it would be so desolate without her," said the first speaker again.

The host nodded, his jaws moving.

"She made the New-Year's punch for us four-and-forty times," continued his friend.

"Yes, it's as long as that since we moved to Berlin, and you became our friend," said the old soldier.

"Last year at this time we were all so jolly together," said the other. "She sat in the armchair there, knitting socks for Paul's eldest. She worked busily, saying she must finish it by twelve o'clock. And she did finish it. Then we drank our punch and spoke quite calmly of death. And two months later they carried her away. As you know, I have written a fat book on the 'Immortality of the Idea.' You never cared much about it—I don't care for it myself now that your wife is dead. The entire Idea of the Universe means nothing to me now."

"Yes, she was a good wife," said the husband of the dead woman; "she cared for me well. When I had to go out for service at five o'clock in the morning, she was always up before me to look after my coffee. Of course she had her faults. When she got into philosophizing with you—h'm."

"You never understood her," murmured the other, the corners of his mouth trembling in controlled resentment. But the glance that rested long on his friend's face was gentle and sad, as if a secret guilt pressed upon his soul.

After a renewed pause, he began:

"Franz, there is something I want to tell you, something that has long troubled me, something that I do not want to carry with me to my grave."

"Well, fire away," said the host, taking up the long pipe that stood beside his chair.

"There was once—something—between your wife and me."

The host let his pipe fall back again, and stared at his friend with wide-opened eyes.

"No jokes, please, doctor," he said finally.

"It is bitter earnest, Franz," replied the other. "I have carried it about with me these forty years, but now it is high time to have it out with you."

"Do you mean to say that the dead woman was untrue to me?" cried the husband angrily.

"For shame, Franz," said his friend with a soft, sad smile.

The old soldier murmured something and lit his pipe.

"No, she was as pure as God's angels," continued the other. "It is you and I who are the guilty ones. Listen to me. It is now forty-three years ago; you had just been ordered here as captain to Berlin, and I was teaching at the University. You were a gay bird then, as you know."

"H'm," remarked the host, raising his trembling old hand to his mustache.

"There was a beautiful actress with great black eyes and little white teeth—do you remember?"

"*Do* I? Bianca was her name," answered the other as a faded smile flashed over his weather-beaten, self-indulgent face. "Those little white teeth could bite, I can tell you."

"You deceived your wife, and she suspected it. But she said nothing and suffered in silence. She was the first woman who had come into my life since my mother's death. She came into it like a shining star, and I gazed up to her in adoration as one might adore a star. I found the courage to ask her about her trouble. She smiled and said that she was not feeling quite strong yet—you remember it was shortly after the birth of your Paul. Then came New-Year's Eve—forty-three years ago to-night. I came in at eight o'clock as usual. She sat over her embroidery and I read aloud to her while we waited for you. One hour after another passed and still you did not come. I saw that she grew more and more uneasy, and began to tremble. I trembled with her. I knew where you were, and I feared you might forget the hour of midnight in the arms of that woman. She had dropped her work; I read no longer. A terrible silence weighed upon us. Then I saw a tear gather under her eyelid and drop slowly down upon the embroidery in her lap. I sprang up to go out and look for you. I felt myself capable of tearing you away from that woman by force. But at the same moment she sprang up also from her seat —this very same place where I am sitting now.

" 'Where are you going?' she cried, terror in every feature. 'I am going to fetch Franz,' I said. And then she screamed aloud: 'For God's sake, *you* stay with me at least—don't *you* forsake me also.'

"And she hurried to me, laid both hands on my shoulders and buried her tear-bedewed face on my breast. I trembled in every fiber, no woman had ever stood so near me before. But I controlled myself, and soothed and comforted her—she was so sadly in need of comfort. You came in soon after. You did not notice my emotion, your cheeks were burning, your eyes heavy with the fatigue of love. Since that evening a change had come over me, a change that frightened me. When I had felt her soft arms around my neck, when I had felt the fragrance of her hair, the shining star fell from its heaven, and—a woman stood before me, beautiful, breathing love. I called myself a villain, a betrayer, and to soothe my conscience somewhat I set about separating you from your mistress. Fortunately I had some money at my disposal. She was satisfied with the sum I offered her, and—"

"The devil!" exclaimed the old soldier in surprise; "then you were the cause of that touching farewel letter that Bianca sent me—in which she declare that she must give me up—altho her heart would break?"

"Yes, I was the cause of it," said his friend. "But listen, there is more to tell. I had thought to purchase peace with that money, but the peace did not come. The wild thoughts ran riot all the more madly in my brain. I buried myself in my work—it was just about that time that I was working out the plan of my book on the 'Immortality of the Idea'—but still could not find peace. And thus the year passed and New-Year's Eve came round again. Again we sat together here, she and I. You were at home this time, but you lay sleeping on the sofa in the next room. A merry Casino dinner had tired you. And as I sat beside her, and my eyes rested on her pale face, then memory came over me with irresistible power. Once more I would feel her head on my breast, once more I would kiss her—and then—the end, if need be. Our eyes met for an instant; I seemed to see a secret understanding, an answer in her glance. I could control myself no longer; I fell at her feet and buried my burning face in her lap.

"I lay there motionless for two seconds perhaps, then I felt her soft hand rest cool upon my head, and her voice, soft and gentle, spoke the words: 'Be brave, dear friend; yes, be brave—do not deceive the man sleeping so trustfully in the next room.' I sprang up and gazed about, bewildered. She took a book from the table and handed it to me. I understood, opened it at random, and began to read aloud. I do not know what it was I read, the letters danced before my eyes

But the storm within my soul began to abate, and when twelve o'clock struck, and you came in sleepily for the New-Year's wishes, it was as if that moment of sin lay far, far behind me, in days that had long passed.

"Since that day I have been calmer. I knew that she did not return my love, and that I had only pity to hope from her. Years passed, your children grew up and married, we three grew old together. You gave up your wild life, forgot the other women, and lived for one alone, as I did. It was not possible that I should ever cease to love her, but my love took on another shape; earthly desires faded, and a bond of the spirit grew up between us. You have often laughed when you heard us philosophizing together. But if you had known how close were our souls at such moments you would have been very jealous. And now she is dead, and before the next New-Year's Eve comes round we two may follow her. It is, therefore, high time that I rid myself of this secret and say to you, 'Franz, I sinned against you once, forgive me.'"

He held out an imploring hand toward his friend; but the other answered, grumbling: "Nonsense. There is nothing to forgive. What you told me there, I knew it long ago. She confessed it herself forty years ago. And now I will tell you why I ran after other women until I was an old man—because she told me then that you were the one and only love of her life."

The friend stared at him without speaking, and the hoarse clock began to strike—midnight.

MADEMOISELLE OLYMPE ZABRISKI

By Thomas Bailey Aldrich

Chapter I

We are accustomed to speak with a certain light
irony of the tendency which women have to gossip, as
if the sin itself, if it is a sin, were of the gentler sex,
and could by no chance be a masculine peccadillo. So
far as my observation goes, men are as much given to
small talk as women, and it is undeniable that we have
produced the highest type of gossiper extant. Where
will you find, in or out of literature, such another
droll, delightful, chatty busybody as Samuel Pepys,
Esq., Secretary to the Admiralty in the reigns of those
fortunate gentlemen Charles II and James II of England? He is the king of tattlers as Shakespeare is the
king of poets.

If it came to a matter of pure gossip, I would back
Our Club against the Sorosis or any women's club in
existence. Whenever you see in our drawing-room four
or five young fellows lounging in easy-chairs, cigar in
hand, and now and then bringing their heads together
over the small round Japanese table which is always
the pivot of these social circles, you may be sure that
they are discussing Tom's engagement, or Dick's ex-
travagance, or Harry's hopeless passion for the younger
Miss Fleurdelys. It is here old Tippleton gets execrated

(Used by permission of and by arrangement with Houghton
Mifflin Co.)

for that everlasting *bon mot* of his which was quite a
success at dinner-parties forty years ago; it is here the
belle of the season passes under the scalpels of merci-
less young surgeons; it is here B's financial condition
is handled in a way that would make B's hair stand on
end; it is here, in short, that everything is canvassed—
everything that happens in our set, I mean, much that
never happens, and a great deal that could not possibly
happen. It was at Our Club that I learned the par-
ticulars of the Van Twiller affair.

It was great entertainment to Our Club, the Van
Twiller affair, tho it was rather a joyless thing, I
fancy, for Van Twiller. To understand the case fully,
it should be understood that Ralph Van Twiller is one
of the proudest and most sensitive men living. He is a
lineal descendant of Wouter Van Twiller, the famous
old Dutch governor of New York—Nieuw Amsterdam,
as it was then; his ancestors have always been burgo-
masters or admirals or generals, and his mother is the
Mrs. Vanrensselaer Vanzandt Van Twiller whose mag-
nificent place will be pointed out to you on the right
bank of the Hudson, as you pass up the historic river
towards Idlewild. Ralph is about twenty-five years old.
Birth made him a gentleman, and the rise of real estate
—some of it in the family since the old governor's time
—made him a millionaire. It was a kindly fairy that
stepped in and made him a good fellow also. Fortune,
I take it, was in her most jocund mood when she
heaped her gifts in this fashion on Van Twiller, who
was, and will be again, when this cloud blows over, the
flower of Our Club.

About a year ago there came a whisper—if the word
"whisper" is not too harsh a term to apply to what
seemed a mere breath floating gently through the

atmosphere of the billiard-room—imparting the intelli-
gence that Van Twiller was in some kind of trouble.
Just as everybody suddenly takes to wearing square-
toed boots, or to drawing his neckscarf through a ring,
so it became all at once the fashion, without any pre-
concerted agreement, for everybody to speak of Van
Twiller as a man in some way under a cloud. But what
the cloud was, and how he got under it, and why he
did not get away from it, were points that lifted themselves into the realm of pure conjecture.   There was
no man in the club with strong enough wing to his
imagination to soar to the supposition that Van Twiller
was embarrassed in money matters. Was he in love?
That appeared nearly as improbable; for if he had been
in love all the world—that is, perhaps a hundred first
families—would have known all about it instantly.

"He has the symptoms," said Delaney, laughing. "I
remember once when Jack Flemming"—

"Ned!" cried Flemming, "I protest against any allu
sion to that business."

This was one night when Van Twiller had wandered
into the club, turned over the magazines absently in the
reading-room, and wandered out again without speaking
ten words.   The most careless eye would have remarked the great change that had come over Van
Twiller.   Now and then he would play a game of
billiards with De Peyster or Haseltine, or stop to chat
a moment in the vestibule with old Duane; but he was
an altered man.   When at the club, he was usually to
be found in the small smoking-room up-stairs, seated
on a fauteuil fast asleep, with the last number of The
Nation in his hand.   Once, if you went to two or three
places of an evening, you were certain to meet Van
Twiller at them all.   You seldom met him in society now.

By and by came whisper number two—a whisper more emphatic than number one, but still untraceable to any tangible mouthpiece. This time the whisper said that Van Twiller *was* in love. But with whom? The list of possible Mrs. Van Twillers was carefully examined by experienced hands, and a check placed against a fine old Knickerbocker name here and there, but nothing satisfactory arrived at. Then that same still small voice of rumor, but now with an easily detected staccato sharpness to it, said that Van Twiller was in love—with an actress! Van Twiller, whom it had taken all these years and all this waste of raw material in the way of ancestors to bring to perfection —Ralph Van Twiller, the net result and flower of his race, the descendant of Wouter, the son of Mrs. Vanrensselaer Vanzandt Van Twiller—in love with an actress! That was too ridiculous to be believed—and so everybody believed it.

Six or seven members of the club abruptly discovered in themselves an unsuspected latent passion for the histrionic art. In squads of two or three they stormed successively all the theater in town—Booth's Wallack's, Daly's Fifth Avenue (not burnt down then), and the Grand Opera House. Even the shabby homes of the drama over in the Bowery, where the Germanic Thespis has not taken out his naturalization papers, underwent rigid exploration. But no clue was found to Van Twiller's mysterious attachment. The *opéra bouffe*, which promised the widest field for investigation, produced absolutely nothing, not even a crop of suspicions. One night, after several weeks of this, Delaney and I fancied that we caught sight of Van Twiller in the private box of an up-town theater, where some thrilling trapeze performance was going on, which we did not care to sit through; but we concluded after wards that it was only somebody who looked like him. Delaney, by the way, was unusually active in this search. I dare say he never quite forgave Van Twiller for calling him Muslin Delaney. Ned is fond of ladies' society, and that's a fact.

The Cimmerian darkness which surrounded Van Twiller's inamorata left us free to indulge in the wildest conjectures. Whether she was black-tressed Melpomene, with bowl and dagger, or Thalia, with the fair hair and the laughing face, was only to be guessed at. It was popularly conceded, however, that Van Twiller was on the point of forming a dreadful *mésalliance*.

Up to this period he had visited the club regularly. Suddenly he ceased to appear. He was not to be seen on Fifth Avenue, or in the Central Park, or at the houses he generally frequented. His chambers—and mighty comfortable chambers they were—on Thirty-fourth Street were deserted. He had dropped out of the world, shot like a bright particular star from his orbit in the heaven of the best society.

The following conversation took place one night in the smoking-room:—

"Where's Van Twiller?"

"Who's seen Van Twiller?"

"What has become of Van Twiller?"

Delaney picked up the Evening Post, and read—with a solemnity that betrayed young Firkins into exclaiming, "By Jove, now!"—

"Married, on the 10th instant, by the Rev. Friar Laurence, at the residence of the bride's uncle, Montague Capulet, Esq., Miss Adrienne Le Couvreur to Mr. Ralph Van Twiller, both of this city. No cards."

"Free List suspended," murmured De Peyster.

"It strikes me," said Frank Livingstone, who had been ruffling the leaves of a magazine at the other end of the table, "that you fellows are in a great fever about Van Twiller."

"So we are."

"Well, he has simply gone out of town."

"Where?"

"Up to the old homestead on the Hudson."

"It's an odd time of year for a fellow to go into the country."

"He has gone to visit his mother," said Livingstone.

"In February?"

"I didn't know, Delaney, that there was any statute in force prohibiting a man from visiting his mother in February if he wants to."

Delaney made some light remark about the pleasure of communing with Nature with a cold in her head, and the topic was dropped.

Livingstone was hand in glove with Van Twiller, and if any man shared his confidence it was Livingstone. He was aware of the gossip and speculation that had been rife in the club, but he either was not at liberty or did not think it worth while to relieve our curiosity. In the course of a week or two it was reported that Van Twiller was going to Europe; and go he did. A dozen of us went down to the Scythia to see him off. It was refreshing to have something as positive as the fact that Van Twiller had sailed.

Chapter II

Shortly after Van Twiller's departure the whole thing came out. Whether Livingstone found the secret too heavy a burden, or whether it transpired through

some indiscretion on the part of Mrs. Vanrensselaer
Vanzandt Van Twiller, I cannot say; but one evening
the entire story was in the possession of the club.

Van Twiller had actually been very deeply interested
—not in an actress, for the legitimate drama was not
her humble walk in life, but—in Mademoiselle Olympe
Zabriski, whose really perilous feats on the trapeze had
astonished New York the year before, tho they had
failed to attract Delaney and me the night we wandered
into the up-town theater on the trail of Van Twiller's
mystery.

That a man like Van Twiller should be fascinated
even for an instant by a common circus-girl seems incredible; but it is always the incredible thing that
happens. Besides, Mademoiselle Olympe was not a
common circus-girl; she was a most daring and startling
gymnaste, with a beauty and a grace of movement that
gave to her audacious performance almost an air of
prudery. Watching her wondrous dexterity and pliant
strength, both exercised without apparent effort, it
seemed the most natural proceeding in the world that
she should do those unpardonable things. She had a
way of melting from one graceful posture into another,
like the dissolving figures thrown from a stereopticon.
She was a lithe, radiant shape out of the Grecian
mythology, now poised up there above the gaslights,
and now gleaming through the air like a slender gilt
arrow.

I am describing Mademoiselle Olympe as she appeared to Van Twiller on the first occasion when he
strolled into the theater where she was performing
To me she was a girl of eighteen or twenty years of
age (maybe she was much older, for pearl-powder and
distance keep these people perpetually young), slightly

but exquisitely built, with sinews of silver wire; rather
pretty, perhaps, after a manner, but showing plainly
the effects of the exhaustive drafts she was making on
her physical vitality. Now, Van Twiller was an en-
thusiast on the subject of calisthenics. "If I had a
daughter," Van Twiller used to say, "I wouldn't send
her to a boarding-school, or a nunnery; I'd send her
to a gymnasium for the first five years. Our American
women have no physique. They are lilies, pallid, pretty
—and perishable. You marry an American woman,
and what do you marry? A headache. Look at Eng-
lish girls. They are at least roses, and last the season
through."

Walking home from the theater that first night, it
flitted through Van Twiller's mind that if he could give
this girl's set of nerves and muscles to any one of the
two hundred high-bred women he knew, he would marry
her on the spot and worship her forever.

The following evening he went to see Mademoiselle
Olympe again. "Olympe Zabriski," he soliloquized, as
he sauntered through the lobby—"what a queer name!
Olympe is French, and Zabriski is Polish. It is her
nom de guerre, of course; her real name is probably
Sarah Jones. What kind of creature can she be in
private life, I wonder? I wonder if she wears that
costume all the time, and if she springs to her meals
from a horizontal bar. Of course she rocks the baby
to sleep on the trapeze." And Van Twiller went on
making comical domestic tableaux of Mademoiselle
Zabriski, like the clever, satirical dog he was, until the
curtain rose.

This was on a Friday. There was a matinée the next
day, and he attended that, tho he had secured a
seat for the usual evening entertainment. Then it be-

came a habit of Van Twiller's to drop into the theater for half an hour or so every night, to assist at the interlude, in which she appeared. He cared only for her part of the program, and timed his visits accordingly. It was a surprize to himself when he reflected, one morning, that he had not missed a single performance of Mademoiselle Olympe for nearly two weeks.

"This will never do," said Van Twiller. "Olympe"— he called her Olympe, as if she were an old acquaintance, and so she might have been considered by that time—"is a wonderful creature; but this will never do. Van, my boy, you must reform this altogether."

But half past nine that night saw him in his accustomed orchestra chair, and so on for another week. A habit leads a man so gently in the beginning that he does not perceive he is led—with what silken threads and down what pleasant avenues it leads him! By and by the soft silk threads become iron chains, and the pleasant avenues Avernus!

Quite a new element had lately entered into Van Twiller's enjoyment of Mademoiselle Olympe's ingenious feats—a vaguely born apprehension that she might slip from that swinging bar; that one of the thin cords supporting it might snap, and let her go headlong from the dizzy height. Now and then, for a terrible instant, he would imagine her lying a glittering, palpitating heap at the foot-lights, with no color in her lips! Sometimes it seemed as if the girl were tempting this kind of fate. It was a hard, bitter life, and nothing but poverty and sordid misery at home could have driven her to it. What if she should end it all some night, by just unclasping that little hand? It looked so small and white from where Van Twiller sat!

This frightful idea fascinated while it chilled him.

and helped to make it nearly impossible for him to keep away from the theater. In the beginning his attendance had not interfered with his social duties or pleasures; but now he came to find it distasteful after dinner to do anything but read, or walk the streets aimlessly, until it was time to go to the play. When that was over, he was in no mood to go anywhere but to his rooms. So he dropped away by insensible degrees from his habitual haunts, was missed, and began to be talked about at the club. Catching some intimation of this, he ventured no more in the orchestra stalls, but shrouded himself behind the draperies of the private box in which Delaney and I thought we saw him on one occasion.

Now, I find it very perplexing to explain what Van Twiller was wholly unable to explain to himself. He was not in love with Mademoiselle Olympe. He had no wish to speak to her, or to hear her speak. Nothing could have been easier, and nothing further from his desire, than to know her personally. A Van Twiller personally acquainted with a strolling female acrobat! Good heavens! That was something possible only with the discovery of perpetual motion. Taken from her theatrical setting, from her lofty perch, so to say, on the trapeze-bar, Olympe Zabriski would have shocked every aristocratic fiber in Van Twiller's body. He was simply fascinated by her marvellous grace and *élan*, and the magnetic recklessness of the girl. It was very young in him and very weak, and no member of the Sorosis, or all the Sorosisters together, could have been more severe on Van Twiller than he was on himself. To be weak, and to know it, is something of a punishment for a proud man. Van Twiller took his punishment, and went to the theater regularly.

"When her engagement comes to an end," he meditated, "that will finish the business."

Mademoiselle Olympe's engagement finally did come to an end, and she departed. But her engagement had been highly beneficial to the treasury-chest of the uptown theater, and before Van Twiller could get over missing her she had returned from a short Western tour, and her immediate reappearance was underlined on the play-bills.

On a dead-wall opposite the windows of Van Twiller's sleeping-room there appeared, as if by necromancy, an aggressive poster with MADEMOISELLE OLYMPE ZABRISKI on it in letters at least a foot high. This thing stared him in the face when he woke up, one morning. It gave him a sensation as if she had called on him overnight, and left her card.

From time to time through the day he regarded that poster with a sardonic eye. He had pitilessly resolved not to repeat the folly of the previous month. To say that this moral victory cost him nothing would be to deprive it of merit. It cost him many internal struggles. It is a fine thing to see a man seizing his temptation by the throat, and wrestling with it, and trampling it under foot like St. Anthony. This was the spectacle Van Twiller was exhibiting to the angels.

The evening Mademoiselle Olympe was to make her reappearance, Van Twiller, having dined at the club, and feeling more like himself than he had felt for weeks, returned to his chamber, and, putting on dressing-gown and slippers, piled up the greater portion of his library about him, and fell to reading assiduously. There is nothing like a quiet evening at home with some slight intellectual occupation, after one's feathers have been stroked the wrong way.

When the lively French clock on the mantel-piece—
a base of malachite surmounted by a flying bronze
Mercury with its arms spread gracefully on the air,
and not remotely suggestive of Mademoiselle Olympe
in the act of executing her grand flight from the trapeze
—when the clock, I repeat, struck nine, Van Twiller
paid no attention to it. That was certainly a triumph.
I am anxious to render Van Twiller all the justice I
can, at this point of the narrative, inasmuch as when
the half hour sounded musically, like a crystal ball
dropping into a silver bowl, he rose from the chair
automatically, thrust his feet into his walking-shoes,
threw his overcoat across his arm, and strode out of
the room.

To be weak and to scorn your weakness, and not to
be able to conquer it, is, as has been said, a hard thing;
and I suspect it was not with unalloyed satisfaction
that Van Twiller found himself taking his seat in the
back part of the private box night after night during
the second engagement of Mademoiselle Olympe. It
was so easy not to stay away!

In this second edition of Van Twiller's fatuity, his
case was even worse than before. He not only thought
of Olympe quite a number of times between breakfast
and dinner, he not only attended the interlude regularly, but he began, in spite of himself, to occupy his
leisure hours at night by dreaming of her. This was
too much of a good thing, and Van Twiller regarded it
so. Besides, the dream was always the same—a har-
rowing dream, a dream singularly adapted to shattering
the nerves of a man like Van Twiller. He would
imagine himself seated at the theater (with all the
members of Our Club in the parquet), watching
Mademoiselle Olympe as usual, when suddenly that

young lady would launch herself desperately from the trapeze, and come flying through the air like a firebrand hurled at his private box. Then the unfortunate man would wake up with cold drops standing on his forehead.

There is one redeeming feature in this infatuation of Van Twiller's which the sober moralist will love to look upon—the serene unconsciousness of the person who caused it. She went through her *rôle* with admirable aplomb, drew her salary, it may be assumed, punctually, and appears from first to last to have been ignorant that there was a miserable slave wearing her chains nightly in the left-hand proscenium-box.

That Van Twiller, haunting the theater with the persistency of an ex-actor, conducted himself so discreetly as not to draw the fire of Mademoiselle Olympe's blue eyes shows that Van Twiller, however deeply under a spell, was not in love. I say this, tho I think if Van Twiller had not been Van Twiller, if he had been a man of no family and no position and no money, if New York had been Paris and Thirty-fourth Street a street in the Latin Quarter—but it is useless to speculate on what might have happened. What did happen is sufficient.

It happened, then, in the second week of Queen Olympe's second unconscious reign, that an appalling Whisper floated up the Hudson, effected a landing at a point between Spuyten Duyvel Creek and Cold Spring, and sought out a stately mansion of Dutch architecture standing on the bank of the river. The Whisper straightway informed the lady dwelling in this mansion that all was not well with the last of the Van Twillers; that he was gradually estranging himself from his peers, and wasting his nights in a play-house watching a misguided young woman turning unmaidenly somersaults on a piece of wood attached to two ropes.

Mrs. Vanrensselaer Vanzandt Van Twiller came down to town by the next train to look into this little matter. She found the flower of the family taking an early breakfast, at 11 A. M. in his cozy apartment on Thirty-fourth Street. With the least possible circumlocution she confronted him with what rumor had reported of his pursuits, and was pleased, but not too much pleased, when he gave her an exact account of his relations with Mademoiselle Zabriski, neither concealing nor qualifying anything. As a confession, it was unique, and might have been a great deal less entertaining. Two or three times in the course of the narrative, the matron had some difficulty in preserving the gravity of her countenance. After meditating a few minutes, she tapped Van Twiller softly on the arm with the tip of her parasol, and invited him to return with her the next day up the Hudson and make a brief visit at the home of his ancestors. He accepted the invitation with outward alacrity and inward disgust.

When this was settled, and the worthy lady had withdrawn, Van Twiller went directly to the establishment of Messrs Ball, Black, and Company, and selected, with unerring taste, the finest diamond bracelet procurable. For his mother? Dear me, no! She had the family jewels.

I would not like to state the enormous sum Van Twiller paid for this bracelet. It was such a clasp of diamonds as would have hastened the pulsation of a patrician wrist. It was such a bracelet as Prince Camaralzaman might have sent to the Princess Badoura, and the Princess Badoura—might have been very glad to get.

In the fragrant Levant morocco case, where these happy jewels lived when they were at home, Van Twiller thoughtfully placed his card, on the back of which he had written a line begging Mademoiselle Olympe Zabriski to accept the accompanying trifle from one who had witnessed her graceful performances with interest and pleasure. This was not done inconsiderately. "Of course I must enclose my card, as I would to any lady," Van Twiller had said to himself. "A Van Twiller can neither write an anonymous letter nor make an anonymous present." Blood entails its duties as well as its privileges.

The casket dispatched to its destination, Van Twiller felt easier in his mind. He was under obligations to the girl for many an agreeable hour that might otherwise have passed heavily. He had paid the debt, and he had paid it *en prince*, as became a Van Twiller. He spent the rest of the day in looking at some pictures at Goupil's, and at the club, and in making a few purchases for his trip up the Hudson. A consciousness that this trip up the Hudson was a disorderly retreat came over him unpleasantly at intervals.

When he returned to his rooms late at night, he found a note lying on the writing-table. He started as his eye caught the words "——— Theater" stamped in carmine letters on one corner of the envelop Van Twiller broke the seal with trembling fingers.

Now, this note some time afterwards fell into the hands of Livingstone, who showed it to Stuyvesant, who showed it to Delaney, who showed it to me, and I copied it as a literary curiosity. The note ran as follows:—

MR VAN TWILLER DEAR SIR—i am verry greatfull to you fo that Bracelett. it come just in the nic of time for me. The Mademoiselle Zabriski dodg is about Plaid out. my beard is getting to much for me. i shall have to grow a mustash and take to some other line of busyness, i dont no what now, but will let you no. You wont feel bad if i sell that Bracelett. i have seen Abrahams Moss and he says he will do the square thing. Pleas accep my thanks for yours Beautifull and Unexpected present.

Youre respectfull servent,
CHARLES MONTMORENCI WALTERS.

The next day Van Twiller neither expressed nor felt any unwillingness to spend a few weeks with his mother at the old homestead.

And then he went abroad.

BOLESS

By Maxim Gorki

An acquaintance of mine once told me the following
story:

"While still a student at Moscow I happened to
be living alongside one of those—well, she was a
Polish woman, Teresa by name. A tall, powerfully
built brunet with heavy, bushy eyebrows, and a large
coarse, vulgar face, as if carved out with an ax—the
animal gleam of her eyes, the deep bass voice, the
gait and manners of a cabman, and her immense
strength like that of a market-woman, inspired me
with an inexpressible horror. I lived in the garret
of the house, and her room was opposite mine. I
never opened my door when I knew that she was in.
But this, of course, happened very rarely. Sometimes
I chanced to meet her on the landing, staircase, or
in the yard, and she would look at me with a smile
which seemed to me cynical and rapacious. Occa-
sionally I saw her in her cups, with bleary eyes, her
hair and clothes in disorder and with a particularly
loathsome smile. On such occasions she would meet
my eye with an impudent stare and say:

" 'How are you, Pan Student?' [1]

"And her stupid laugh would increase my dislike

[1] Pan is Polish for Mister.

for her still more. I would have liked nothing better
than to change my quarters in order to get rid of her
proximity, but my room was so nice, and the view
from my window was so fine, the street below so
quiet and peaceful, that I concluded to endure it.

"One morning after I had dressed and was sprawling
on the cot, trying to invent some sort of an excuse
for not attending my classes, the door of my room
suddenly opened, and the disgusting bass voice of the
Polish woman sounded from the threshold:

" 'Good morning, Pan Student!'

" 'What is it you wish?' I asked her. I saw she
looked confused and had in her face a kind of pleading
expression, something unusual with her.

" 'You see, Pan Student, I came to beg you to do
me a great favor. Don't refuse me, please!'

"Lying there on my cot I thought that it was just
some pretext or other to make my further acquaintance. Take care, my boy!

" 'You see, I have to send a letter to my native
country,' she continued in a supplicating, low, tremulous
voice.

" 'Well,' I thought, 'the devil take you. If you
wish I will write it for you.' And springing to my feet
I sat down to the table, took some paper and said:
'Well, come nearer; sit down and dictate.'

"She came over; sat down cautiously on the edge
of the chair and looked at me in rather a guilty way.

" 'To whom shall I write?'

" 'To Boleslav Kapshat, in the town Sventsiani, on
the Warsaw railroad.'

" 'Well, what shall I write? Speak.'

" 'My dearest Boless, my heart's delight, my beloved.

May the Mother of God protect you! My golden
heart, why have you not written for so long a time
to your sorrowing dove, Teresa—'

"I could hardly keep from laughing. A sorrowing
dove, indeed! Almost six feet tall, with the fists
of a prize-fighter, and a face so black that it seemed
as if the 'dove' had been sweeping chimneys all her life
and had never thoroughly washed herself. But I
somehow kept my face straight and asked:

" 'Who is this Bolesst?'

" 'Boless, Pan Student,' she replied, seemingly
offended because of my mispronouncing the name. 'He
is my affianced.'

" 'Affianced!'

" 'And why are you so astonished? Can not I,
a girl, have an affianced?'

"She—a girl! well, this beats everything I ever
heard. Oh, well, who can tell about such matters!
Everything is possible in this world.

" 'And have you been long engaged?'

" 'The sixth year.'

" 'Oh, oh!' I thought and then said aloud: 'Well, go
ahead with your letter.'

"And I must confess—so tender and loving was this
message—that I would have willingly exchanged places
with this Boless had the fair correspondent been any
one else but Teresa.

" 'I thank you from my inmost soul for your favor,
Pan Student,' Teresa said, bowing low. 'Can I in
any way be of service to you?'

" 'No thank you.'

" 'But maybe the Pan's shirts or trousers need
mending?'

"This made me quite angry. I felt that this masto

so hard for you to draw a few lines on the paper!
Oh, you! And I thought you such a good fellow,
such a nice fair-haired little boy. Yes, it is true—
there is no Boless, and there is no Teresa, there is only
me! Well, what of it?'

"'Allow me,' I said greatly disconcerted by this
reception. 'What is it you are saying? Is there no
Boless?'

"'Yes, there is none. But what of it?'

"'And no Teresa either?'

"'No, no Teresa either; that is, yes, I am her.

"I could not understand a word. I stared straight
into her eyes, trying to determine which of us two
had lost our reason. And she returned once more to
the table, rummaged for some time in the drawer, and
coming back to me said in an offended tone:

"'Here is the letter you wrote for me, take it back.
You do not wish to write me a second one anyway.
Others will probably be kinder than you and would
do so.'

"I recognized the letter she held out to me as the
one I wrote for her to Boless. Humph!

"'Look here, Teresa,' I said to her. 'Will you
please explain to me what it all means? Why do
you ask people to write letters for you when you
do not find it necessary even to post them?'

"'Post them? Where to?'

"'Why, to this Boless, of course.'

"'But he does not exist!'

"I really could not understand a word. There
was nothing left for me to do but to spit and walk
out of the room. But she explained herself.

"'Well, what of it?' she began in an offended voice.
'He does not exist. He does not, so,' and she extended

her hands as if she could not herself clearly understand why he did not exist in reality. 'But I want him to. Am I not as much of a human being as the others? Of course I—I know— But it does no harm to any one, that I am writing to him—'

" 'Allow me—to whom?'

" 'To Boless, of course.'

" 'But he does not exist.'

' 'Oh, Mother of God! What if he does not exist? He does not; still to me he does. And Teresa—this is myself, and he replies to my letters, and I write to him again.

"I understood. I felt so sick at heart, so ashamed of myself to know that alongside of me, only three paces removed, lived a human being who had no one in the whole world to love and sympathize with her, and that this being had to invent a friend for herself.

" Here you have written a letter from me to Boless, and I gave it to another to read, and when I hear it read it really begins to seem to me as if there is a Boless. And then I ask that a letter be written from Boless to Teresa—that is to me. And when such a letter is written and is read to me then I am almost entirely convinced that there is a Boless, and that makes my life easier.'

"Yes, the devil take it all," continued my acquaintance. "To make a long story short I began from that time on to write with the greatest punctuality twice a week letters to Boless and vice versa. I wrote splendid replies to her. She used to listen to my reading of those epistles and to weep in her bass voice. In return for this she used to mend my clothes and darn my socks.

"Three months later she was thrown into prison

for some reason or other and by now she must surely be dead."

My acquaintance blew the ashes from his cigaret, looked thoughtfully at the sky, and concluded:

"Y-e-s, the more a human being has drunk of the cup of bitterness the more ardently he longs for sweetness. And we, enveloped in our worn-out virtues and gazing at each other through the haze of self-sufficiency and convinced of our righteousness, fail to understand it.

"And the whole affair turns out very stupid, and very cruel. Fallen people we say—but whc and what are those fallen ones? First of all they are human beings of the very same bone and blood, of the very same flesh and nerves as ourselves. We have been told the very same thing for whole ages, day in and day out. And we listen and—and the devil alone knows how stupid it all is! In reality we, too, are but fallen people and more deeply fallen too, probably —into the abyss of self-sufficiency, convinced of our own sinlessness and superiority, the superiority of our own nerves and brains over the nerves and brains of those who are only less crafty than we are, and who can not, as we can, feign a goodness they do not possess—but enough of this. It is all so old and stale—so old and stale indeed that one is ashamed to speak of it—"

A POSTSCRIPT TO DIVORCE

By Gouverneur Morris

Their names were Park and Erskine, and they had been shot out of the main stream of life and were aimlessly drifting around and around and hither and yonder in one of those warm and pleasant eddies upon which the sun nearly always shines. They were middle-aged men, gray-haired, with well-tanned faces, and the golf which they played every afternoon over the Del Norte course would probably keep them so for years to come.

They were supposed to be rich. The caddies knew them to be tolerant and generous. At golf they were very evenly matched, and on their best days played in the late eighties. Each had come to Del Norte with the idea of spending a few days only. That had been during the month when California suddenly explodes into wild flowers, and they had lingered on into the summer, and through the summer. They had then made the discovery that the very best of all the months at Del Norte are September, October and November. A little rain fell then—only enough to improve the golf and freshen the vegetation; and they still lingered. They said, "Why bother to go away now? In another month it will begin to be spring."

They were shy, reticent men. It is doubtful if either would ever have introduced himself to the other.

(From *"Hearst's International"*; copyright, 1924, by International Publications, Inc.)

But the professional introduced them and the first round of golf that they played together finishing all even, they agreed to continue it on the following day. After they had played together thirty or forty times they began to feel as if they were friends and they made the pleasant discovery that their respective codes of conduct and philosophies of life were immensely compatible.

They became fixtures at the Del Norte. They shared a table in the vast dining room, visited the barber shop at the same times, and were seldom far apart. Now any marked line of conduct long persisted in is bound in the end to enjoy a local celebrity. If the humblest woman in the village makes consistently good tamales and enchilada she becomes celebrated; so with the village drunkard, and the village cut-up.

The gentleness, the urbanity, the attentiveness and good manners of Park and Erskine were first noticed by the professional at the golf club, the caddy master and the caddies. Then the management of the hotel discovered their quality and laid itself out to please. Then became known to the half-dozen old-timers who had lived in the hotel ever since anybody could remember; and finally their celebrity leaked out into the village, and when they had shopping to do they were always better and more affectionately waited on than anybody else.

But nobody really knew anything about them. They came from so very far off—from New York or Philadelphia or some other old place which once had been a part of America.

In their day Park and Erskine had sometimes drunk a cocktail before dinner, champagne with the dinner and perhaps a whisky and soda or so afterward. But there was no record of dissipation written upon the face of either one, and if there had been no such thing as alcohol in the world they would have lived out the rest of their lives with discomfort. And both had acquired a taste for Scotch whisky.

As this particular brand of whisky is more widely distributed throughout the country than it used to be, they had no trouble to keep a stock in their bedrooms, and almost every day after golf and after dinner they had a few drinks together. Otherwise they might never have learned anything important about each other.

It was Scotch which emboldened Erskine to ask Park about the photograph of the two pretty girls on his bureau. They were Park's daughters. One was just married and the other was going to be. Not to be outdone, Erskine admitted to having two daughters of his own—charming girls, and both about to be married.

But it was not until the night of Washington's Birthday that the two friends, having drunk a little too much Scotch, dined rosily in the grill and about ten o'clock, returning to Park's room to have a few more drinks, became really confidential. They had been friends then for nearly four years.

"Do you ever get things like this?" Park asked. And he showed Erskine a telegram. It was the request of an ingenious daughter named Margaret for a sum of money.

"Oh yes," said Erskine, "often! But *my* youngsters write. They don't telegraph."

"Mine don't," said Park, "only every now and then —every once in a great while." He sighed, poured whisky into two little glasses and lifted one to his lips. "To the good old days," he said, "when there was more to drink in America and less drinking."

Erskine drank the toast, but being in a single-minded state, induced by liquor, was not ready to be side-tracked from the subject of his daughters. His heart felt very warm toward them and he missed them with a great and sudden aching of the spirit.

"My daughters are very, very good to me," he said. "They have been ever since they were born. They have never forgiven their mother for separating us—"

"Wonderful!" exclaimed Park. "The power they give the women."

"Fearful and wonderful," Erskine agreed, but still I incline to think that after separation or divorce it is the best guess to leave the children—especially if they are girls—with the mother."

"We've known each other pretty well now for some time," said Park. "That emboldens me to ask if you are divorced."

"I would have told you so long ago if I had thought you would be interested. There is no secret about it. It was in the papers at the time—not a celebrated case of course, but I am sorry to say we were on the front page twice. Fortunately the children were little. All they know is that their mother divorced me and kept them with her. But it was a hard break-up for them—poor dears—they and their daddy were very close . . ."

"My babies and I," remarked Park sadly, "were very close too. I am also divorced, you know. Mean business to go through, isn't it?" He poured whisky into two glasses and looking at Erskine with real affection said: "Old man, I can understand how a woman would get sick to death of living with me; but how one could ever find fault with a man of your open-handed, kind-hearted disposition—well, that beats me."

"Oh," said Erskine, "she thought that she would be happier with another man!"

"That's what mine thought," said Park.

"And that," said Erskine with emphasis, "is what they all think—at times. Our grandmothers thought it, most of them. But they hadn't access to the facile destructive agencies of today. And they kept their thoughts to themselves. It was only once in a great while that they ever shared them with the other man. Nowadays, the minute a wife has chosen another man——"

"She tells him," interrupted Park.

"Not in the best circles," said Erskine. "She makes him tell her. And nine times out of ten she's so elated over that that she rushes right off and tells her husband too. It's a superb situation for a woman—full of drama and fate and never and forever. She sees herself caught in an institution from which there is no escape—beyond the bars she sees love and romance —the real thing—not the thing her husband gave her— no—not ever—not even when they were boy and girl together and drifted sweetly and inevitably and at the same time sanely into a lifelong partnership. Caught in the institution, she for a while delights in the thought that escape is impossible. She delights in the thought of enduring the greatest unhappiness that has ever been endured. When she has enjoyed this kind of thing to her heart's content, she begins to talk about her duty to herself. Every crime that is committed in the world is a sure proof that some man or woman has been doing his or her duty by his or her self. But women are almost more thorough about it than men."

"I have thought just such thoughts, thousands of times."

"Did your wife say that she would kill herself if you didn't let her go free?"

"Of course."

"So did mine."

"Did you believe yours?"

"No. But I didn't dare run the one risk in a million that she was speaking the truth."

"Neither did I. Did yours go off her feed and get dark circles under her eyes and look so wobegone and martyred and pathetic that you felt like shooting yourself?"

"You describe my ex as accurately as if you had seen her. But as a matter of fact she snitched things in the pantry between meals and the rest was make-up. The dark circles would have come off on a rough towel."

"But they get punished in the end," said Erskine. "Always?"

"Always, I should say—if there are children. Just think how things were with us. We had a house on Long Island, a house at Newport, another with very fine shooting near Thomasville, Georgia, and an apartment in town. We had money enough to move ourselves, servants and horses from one place to the other according to the seasons. My wife always had more clothes than she could wear and was always buying more. We had friends whom it would have been comfortable to grow old with; and our little daughters were beginning to make the right kind of friendships and associations. The children were particularly happy in the kind of life they were able to live—always out of-doors, learning to ride and to shoot and to swim and to sail—learning to be good sports—not to show too much grief when they lost or too much self-satis-faction when they won. They adored their mother and they adored me. It was never any trouble to make them obey. We never had to punish them Speaking the truth was second nature to them."

"A little drop wouldn't hurt you——"

"Thanks. I believe this is the best Scotch we have had—the smoothest."

"That Perfection was pretty good too."

The gentlemen drank and Park said:

"I suppose we've both got a lot to make us miser-able and at the same time a lot to make us thankful. I suppose we could even marry again if we wanted to; and there's the golf and the climate and the fact that we are close to the sea—no trouble getting drinks—and that we have enough money."

"Oh," said Erskine, "I hope I'm thankful! I make it a principle never to think about the men who have had better luck than I've had, but about the men who've had worse. But there's always a kind of ache. It's a mean feeling—this being thrown out on the rubbish heap. And then all the regrets for the mis-takes."

"You made mistakes too?"

"And if I had it to go through again I'd make mis-takes. Not the same ones perhaps, but others. A woman gets a man into a certain situation and any-thing that he does is a mistake. If he is patient she takes more liberty, if he is stern she makes it appear. even in his own eyes, that he is cruel. But I hold it as an axiom that no man who does not deserve to

be divorced ought to allow himself to be divorced
and separated from his children. I wouldn't make
that mistake again."

"You would divorce Mrs. Erskine?"

"I wouldn't let her divorce me."

"Were you divorced—back East?"

"Do you mean," asked Erskine, "was I divorced
upon the only grounds which are allowed in the New
York statutes? Yes. I was. And I was a man who
had never looked at any woman but his wife and who
had never wanted to! That part was funny, tho."

Park wondered if he dared ask Erskine a question.
He dared, his eyes twinkling:

"Did you really furnish grounds?"

Erskine shook his head. "It was my intention,"
he said. "I didn't want to be jailed for conspiracy
right on top of all the other troubles. But I didn't.
The young lady whom I finally selected to be in love
with turned out to be such a square straight shooter
and such a pleasant and amiable companion that I
couldn't help respecting her. She—well, her father
had been in the wine business, and prohibition had
ruined him, and she was willing to go to any lengths
to get a little capital and set him on his feet. So she
gave her name to a lady who has a good deal to do
with a good many New York City divorces, and my
lawyer introduced me to this lady and she introduced
me to the girl. Do you remember the other day I
spoke to an old man and a young woman in the lobby,
and you asked me who they were?"

"Fine-looking, rosy old man—girl with straight black
bobbed hair and fine eyes. I remember."

"Well, that was the ex-wine merchant and the
daughter who thought less of her own honor than of

his material welfare. I got very interested in her and gave her a good deal more money than was in the bargain."

"They looked very prosperous."

"They are. She told me that they went to Washington and formed a bootlegging partnership—very exclusive—very safe. At the end of three years they were rich. They went out of business and put their money into tax-exempt bonds. Now they travel and live handsomely on their income."

"She had a lot of looks," said Park.

"She has a lot of heart," said Erskine. "She will make some man a very good wife. We managed to keep her name out of the records. I took a room in a little downtown hotel and arranged to have the girl meet me there at a quarter to two in the morning and for my wife's lawyer and detectives to break in upon us a quarter of an hour later—that was all there was to it. And I was divorced and my wife was awarded the custody of the children and whatever else she wanted in the way of alimony.

"But the whole thing was a ghastly mistake. Some intuition told the children that it was not their father who had done them wrong but their mother. And they have never forgiven her. They didn't like the other man at all. They felt that he was their enemy and their father's. They begged me to take them away, and of course that is just what I should have done in the first place; but it was too late. I hadn't the right to do it. It would have been kidnaping under the law. And now they are both about to be married. How time passes!"

"Shall you go East for the weddings?"

"No. It's to be a double wedding and they are

coming to California for their honeymoons. Their mother doesn't like that; but they can do as they please now and they please to do that. We must try to shake off some of our years, Park, and give the youngsters a good time."

As the time for the arrival of the honeymooners drew near, Erskine, always so shy and reserved, began to make quite a show of himself. And Park, tho he tried to be enthusiastic, became more reserved and shy than ever.

Erskine had told the management that his daughters had been married and were bringing their husbands to visit him. He bespoke the choicest rooms in the hotel for them and had them repapered and decorated at his own expense. He made a trip to San Francisco and returned with certain small parcels which he had placed for safe-keeping in the hotel safe. He bought two expensive high-powered roadsters, exactly alike. At the golf club he asked a total stranger if he would mind changing the locker he had been given for another just as good.

"You see," he said, "my daughters have just been married and they are bringing their husbands all the way to California to visit me. And as they all play golf I thought it would be nice if I could get them four lockers all in a row, and the caddy master says that if you are willing to change it can be managed."

One day as Park and Erskine were just leaving the hotel for the golf club, Erskine stepped suddenly in front of an automobile and was almost run over. The people in the automobile apologized, tho it wasn't their fault, and Erskine apologized, profusely.

"You see," he said, "my daughters have just been married and they are bringing their husbands all the

way to California to visit me—and I am so happy
about it that half the time I don't seem to look where
I am going."

Later that same day when the friends came to the
fourteenth hole—a one-shot hole with a dreadful abyss
in front of the green—Park dropped a pretty mashie
shot somewhere in the neighborhood of the pin, while
Erskine dropped a half hit ball into the abyss.

They walked forward together with Erskine chatting
explanations to his caddy.

"You know how it is yourself," he said. "When
you can't put your mind on a shot you can't make
it properly. You see, my two daughters have just been
married and they are bringing their husbands all the
way to California to visit me. They could have gone
to Europe if they preferred. But they prefererd to
come out here to see their father, and that makes me
so happy that I can't seem to concentrate, and I seem
to be all the time looking up."

It may be that Park became a little cool toward his
friend; he was being too often reminded of his own
daughters, who as it happened were not on their way
to see him. Perhaps he was a little jealous of Erskine.
At any rate he develope¹ a faculty for laying short
approaches close to the hole and dropping uncanny
putts into it which afforded him moments of hostile
satisfaction.

Erskine might have his daughters, but he, Park,
was about to have a game of golf.

In all the plans which Erskine was making to entertain his daughters and his sons-in-law Park was in-
cluded. Dear old Park! It would never do to let
him feel slighted or in the way. He was a charming
old fellow—except of course when he was sinking a

long putt; then his charm failed him a little, perhaps. But one forgave him readily because he never rubbed his victories in.

When the young people finally came they were in that joyous and ecstatic state with which so many American marriages begin. There had been no misunderstandings or quarrels. For each of the women there was but one man in the whole world, and for each of the men but the one woman.

Erskine was delighted with his sons-in-law, and Park admitted them to be "nice mannerly boys."

But perhaps it wasn't easy for him to be in the midst of so much happiness of which he was not a part. Erskine was so happy that he looked ten years younger. His daughters' love for him was very warm and very real. They had plenty of room for it side by side with the love that they had for their husbands. Dad was an old peach! Wasn't he, tho!

Saturday came and Erskine gave a dinner party in the grill of the hotel.

At the last moment Park backed out. He said that he wasn't feeling very well. Dinner over and the dancing in full swing, Erskine excused himself.

"I'll just run upstairs," he said, "and see how old Park is getting on. He wasn't feeling any too well this afternoon."

Park was feeling better. He had his collar unbuttoned, his feet up, a quarter of a bottle of sound Scotch whisky inside of him and the rest of the bottle waiting patiently to be drunk. He had started in to drink because he was feeling depressed and unhappy. That mood was passing.

"You're just in time," he said. "I was about to indulge in a nightcap."

"Feeling all right?"

"Feeling fine. And how is the happy father feeling?"

Erskine had a sudden understanding.

"My dear boy," he said, "I've been a pig. I've been rubbing my selfish happiness into you these last weeks so that you must hate the sight of me."

If there remained any bitterness in Park it vanished on the instant. "I love to see people happy," he remarked.

"If only you could have your girls with you."

Park made a gesture of resignation. "You told me all about your divorce," he said, "but I never told you about mine, did I?"

"Only that you had been divorced."

"I didn't mean it that way. I divorced her. When you told me how you had stepped out and furnished grounds and given your wife everything she asked for, I didn't make any comment, did I? But I thought to myself, not what a noble, unselfish fellow you were, but how wise. See how it has worked out. You effaced yourself, you allowed yourself to be put in the wrong, you bore the whole weight of opprobrium, and your daughters saw through the whole thing and they have never forgiven the woman who so hurt them and their father.

"Now our cases are as alike as two peas.

"I give you my word of honor that there was no major reproach to be laid at my door. I loved my wife and I had been faithful to her in word and deed. There was the usual history of other men, and then one other man. She threatened to kill herself if I wouldn't let her get a divorce. I said: 'All right. Kill yourself. Go and jump out of the window, or if you prefer there's an automatic in the top drawer of my bureau among the neckties. Bring it down to me and I'll show you how to work it.'

"What do you suppose she said?"

"I think I know," said Erskine with a faint smile. "I think she said 'You'll be sorry for this' and flounced out of the room."

Park put back his head and laughed heartily—for the first time in weeks. "That," he said, "is exactly what she did say. And she was right. She made me sorry."

He shrugged his shoulders.

"I don't think I need to say more than that," he continued. "But she made me too sorry. And I went to a lawyer, and when the time came—well, I had her cold. The court said that she was not fit to have the custody of her children and they were given to me. I took them abroad. And they kept the memory of their mother alive and beautiful. They made a fetish of it. You might have thought that she was an angel in heaven instead of an enemy of society and a home-wrecker. Little as they were, they began to judge me and turn against me. Forgive me for saying so, old man; but what you did was in flagrant defiance of the law, and you were rewarded. Your children have never forgiven her. I did what was right, and my children have never forgiven me. I had to send them back to her after a while. And now they don't even write."

Erskine rose and laid his hand on Park's shoulder.

"I *am* sorry," he said. "Won't you come down to the grill? It looks very gay tonight. When my daughters go away I'll be just as miserable as you are, if that's any comfort . . ."

"We might have another drink," said Park.

"So we might," said Erskine.

They had it.

"I'll tell you what we might do," said Erskine. "We're not too old to think about romance and happiness. We might hunt up a couple of pretty widows and court them."

But Park shook his head with an air of dismal finality.

"I'll tell you what we *will* do," he said, "like the weak, drifting, inefficient, ageing old fools that we are."

"What?" asked Erskine.

"Golf as usual," said Park.

THE GOLDEN HONEYMOON

By Ring Lardner

Mother says that when I start talking I never know when to stop. But I tell her the only time I get a chance is when she ain't around, so I have to make the most of it. I guess the fact is neither one of us would be welcome in a Quaker meeting, but as I tell Mother, what did God give us tongues for if He didn't want we should use them? Only she says He didn't give them to us to say the same thing over and over again, like I do, and repeat myself. But I say:

"Well, Mother," I say, "when people is like you and I and been married fifty years, do you expect everything I say will be something you ain't heard me say before? But it may be new to others, as they ain't nobody else lived with me as long as you have."

So she says:

"You can bet they ain't, as they couldn't nobody else stand you that long."

"Well," I tell her, "you look pretty healthy."

"Maybe I do," she will say, "but I looked even healthier before I married you."

You can't get ahead of Mother.

Yes, sir, we was married just fifty years ago the seventeenth day of last December and my daughter and son-in-law was over from Trenton to help us celebrate the Golden Wedding. My son-in-law is

136

John H. Kramer, the real estate man. He made $12,000 one year and is pretty well thought of around Trenton; a good, steady, hard worker. The Rotarians was after him a long time to join, but he kept telling them his home was his club. But Edie finally made him join. That's my daughter.

Well, anyway, they come over to help us celebrate the Golden Wedding and it was pretty crimpy weather and the furnace don't seem to heat up no more like it used to and Mother made the remark that she hoped this winter wouldn't be as cold as the last, referring to the winter previous. So Edie said if she was us, and nothing to keep us home, she certainly wouldn't spend no more winters up here and why didn't we just shut off the water and close up the house and go down to Tampa, Florida? You know we was there four winters ago and staid five weeks, but it cost us over three hundred and fifty dollars for hotel bill alone. So Mother said we wasn't going no place to be robbed. So my son-in-law spoke up and said that Tampa wasn't the only place in the South, and besides we didn't have to stop at no high price hotel but could rent us a couple rooms and board out some-wheres, and he had heard that St. Petersburg, Florida, was *the* spot and if we said the word he would write down there and make inquiries.

Well, to make a long story short, we decided to do it and Edie said it would be our Golden Honeymoon and for a present my son-in-law paid the difference between a section and a compartment so as we could have a compartment and have more privatecy. In a compartment you have an upper and lower berth just like the regular sleeper, but it is a shut-in room by itself and got a wash bowl. The car we went in was all compartments and no regular berths at all. It was all compartments.

We went to Trenton the night before and staid at my daughter and son-in-law and we left Trenton the next afternoon at 3.23 P. M.

This was the twelfth day of January. Mother set facing the front of the train, as it makes her giddy to ride backwards. I set facing her, which does not affect me. We reached North Philadelphia at 4.03 P. M. and we reached West Philadelphia at 4.14, but did not go into Broad Street. We reached Baltimore at 6.30 and Washington, D. C., at 7.25. Our train laid over in Washington two hours till another train come along to pick us up and I got out and strolled up the platform and into the Union Station. When I come back, our car had been switched on to another track, but I remembered the name of it, the La Belle, as I had once visited my aunt out in Oconomowoc, Wisconsin, where there was a lake of that name, so I had no difficulty in getting located. But Mother had nearly fretted herself sick for fear I would be left.

"Well," I said, "I would of followed you on the next train."

"You could of," said Mother, and she pointed out that she had the money.

"Well," I said, "we are in Washington and I could of borrowed from the United States Treasury. I would of pretended I was an Englishman."

Mother caught the point and laughed heartily.

Our train pulled out of Washington at 9.40 P. M. and Mother and I turned in early, I taking the upper. During the night we passed through the green fields of old Virginia, tho it was too dark to tell if they was green or what color. When we got up in the morning, we was at Fayetteville, North Carolina. We had breakfast in the dining car and after breakfast I got in conversation with the man in the next compartment to ours. He was from Lebanon, New Hampshire, and a man about eighty years of age. His wife was with him, and two unmarried daughters and I made the remark that I should think the four of them would be crowded in one compartment, but he said they had made the trip every winter for fifteen years and knowed how to keep out of each other's way. He said they was bound for Tarpon Springs.

We reached Charleston, South Carolina, at 12.50 P. M. and arrived at Savannah, Georgia, at 4.20. We reached Jacksonville, Florida, at 8.45 P. M. and had an hour and a quarter to lay over there, but Mother made a fuss about me getting off the train, so we had the darky make up our berths and retired before we left Jacksonville. I didn't sleep good as the train done a lot of hemming and hawing, and Mother never sleeps good on a train as she says she is always worrying that I will fall out. She says she would rather have the upper herself, as then she would not have to worry about me, but I tell her I can't take the risk of having it get out that I allowed my wife to sleep in an upper berth. It would make talk.

We was up in the morning in time to see our friends from New Hampshire get off at Tarpon Springs, which we reached at 6.53 A. M.

Several of our fellow passengers got off at Clearwater and some at Belleair, where the train backs right up to the door of the mammoth hotel. Belleair is the winter headquarters for the golf dudes and everybody that got off there had their bag of sticks, as many as ten and twelve in a bag. Women and all. When I was a young man we called it shinny and only needed one club to play with and about one game of it would of been a-plenty for some of these dudes, the way we played it.

The train pulled into St. Petersburg at 8.20 and when we got off the train you would think they was a riot, what with all the darkies barking for the different hotels.

I said to Mother, I said:

"It is a good thing we have got a place picked out to go to and don't have to choose a hotel, as it would be hard to choose amongst them if every one of them is the best."

She laughed.

We found a jitney and I give him the address of the room my son-in-law had got for us and soon we was there and introduced ourselves to the lady that owns the house, a young widow about forty-eight years of age. She showed us our room, which was light and airy with a comfortable bed and bureau and washstand. It was twelve dollars a week, but the location was good, only three blocks from Williams Park.

St. Pete is what folks calls the town, tho they also call it the Sunshine City, as they claim they's no other place in the country where they's fewer days when Old Sol don't smile down on Mother Earth, and one of the newspapers gives away all their copies free every day when the sun don't shine. They claim to of only give them away some sixty-odd times in the last eleven years. Another nickname they have got for the town is "the Poor Man's Palm Beach," but I guess they's men that comes there that could borrow as much from the bank as some of the Willie boys over to the other Palm Beach.

During our stay we paid a visit to the Lewis Tent City, which is the headquarters for the Tin Can Tourists. But maybe you ain't heard about them. Well, they are an organization that takes their vacation trips by auto and carries everything with them. That is, they bring along their tents to sleep in and cook in and they don't patronize no hotels or cafeterias, but they have got to be bona fide auto campers or they can't belong to the organization.

They tell me they's over 200,000 members to it and they call themselves the Tin Canners on account of most of their food being put up in tin cans. One couple we seen in the Tent City was a couple from Brady, Texas, named Mr. and Mrs. Pence, which the old man is over eighty years of age and they had came in their auto all the way from home, a distance of 1,641 miles. They took five weeks for the trip, Mr. Pence driving the entire distance.

The Tin Canners hails from every State in the Union and in the summer time they visit places like New England and the Great Lakes region, but in the winter the most of them comes to Florida and scatters all over the State. While we was down there, they was a national convention of them at Gainesville, Florida, and they elected a Fredonia, New York, man as their president. His title is Royal Tin Can Opener of the World. They have got a song wrote up which everybody has got to learn it before they are a member:

> "The tin can forever! Hurrah, boys! Hurrah!
> Up with the tin can! Down with the foe!
> We will rally round the campfire, we'll rally once again,
> Shouting, 'We auto camp forever!'"

That is something like it. And the members has also

got to have a tin can fastened on to the front of their machine.

I asked Mother how she would like to travel around that way and she said:

"Fine, but not with an old rattle brain like you driving."

"Well," I said, "I am eight years younger than this Mr. Pence who drove here from Texas."

"Yes," she said, " but he is old enough to not be skittish."

You can't get ahead of Mother.

Well, one of the first things we done in St. Petersburg was to go to the Chamber of Commerce and register our names and where we was from as they's great rivalry amongst the different States in regards to the number of their citizens visiting in town and of course our little State don't stand much of a show, but still every little bit helps, as the fella says. All and all, the man told us, they was eleven thousand names registered, Ohio leading with some fifteen hundred-odd and New York State next with twelve hundred. Then come Michigan, Pennsylvania and so on down, with one man each from Cuba and Nevada.

The first night we was there, they was a meeting of the New York-New Jersey Society at the Congregational Church and a man from Ogdensburg, New York State, made the talk. His subject was Rainbow Chasing. He is a Rotarian and a very convicting speaker, tho I forget his name.

Our first business, of course, was to find a place to eat and after trying several places we run on to a cafeteria on Central Avenue that suited us up and down. We eat pretty near all our meals there and it averaged about two dollars per day for the two of us,

but the food was well cooked and everything nice
and clean. A man don't mind paying the price if
things is clean and well cooked.

On the third day of February, which is Mother's
birthday, we spread ourselves and eat supper at the
Poinsettia Hotel and they charged us seventy-five
cents for a sirloin steak that wasn't hardly big enough
for one.

I said to Mother: "Well," I said, "I guess it's a
good thing every day ain't your birthday or we would
be in the poorhouse."

"No," says Mother, " because if every day was my
birthday, I would be old enough by this time to of
been in my grave long ago."

You can't get ahead of Mother.

In the hotel they had a card-room where they was
several men and ladies playing five hundred and this
new-fangled whist bridge. We also seen a place where
they was dancing, so I asked Mother would she like
to trip the light fantastic toe and she said no, she
was too old to squirm like you have got to do now
days. We watched some of the young folks at it
awhile till Mother got disgusted and said we would
have to see a good movie to take the taste out of our
mouth. Mother is a great movie heroyne and we go
twice a week here at home.

But I want to tell you about the Park. The second
day we was there we visited the Park, which is a
good deal like the one in Tampa, only bigger, and
they's more fun goes on here every day than you
could shake a stick at. In the middle they's a big
bandstand and chairs for the folks to set and listen
to the concerts, which they give you music for all

tastes, from Dixie up to classical pieces like Hearts
and Flowers.

Then all around they's places marked off for different sports and games—chess and checkers and dominos
for folks that enjoys those kind of games, and roque
and horse-shoes for the nimbler ones. I used to pitch
a pretty fair shoe myself, but ain't done much of it
in the last twenty years.

Well, anyway, we bought a membership ticket in
the club which costs one dollar for the season, and
they tell me that up to a couple years ago it was
fifty cents, but they had to raise it to keep out the
riffraff.

Well, Mother and I put in a great day watching
the pitchers and she wanted I should get in the game,
but I told her I was all out of practise and would
make a fool of myself, tho I seen several men pitching who I guess I could take their measure without
practise. However, they was some good pitchers, too,
and one boy from Akron, Ohio, who could certainly
throw a pretty shoe. They told me it looked like
he would win the championship of the United States
in the February tournament. We come away a few
days before they held that and I never did hear if he
win. I forget his name, but he was a clean cut young
fella and he has got a brother in Cleveland that's a
Rotarian.

Well, we just stood around and watched the different games for two or three days and finally I set
down in a checker game with a man named Weaver
from Danville, Illinois. He was a pretty fair checker
player, but he wasn't no match for me, and I hope
that don't sound like bragging. But I always could
hold my own on a checker-board and the folks round

here will tell you the same thing. I played with this
Weaver pretty near all morning for two or three
mornings and he beat me one game and the only
other time it looked like he had a chance, the noon
whistle blowed and we had to quit and go to dinner.

While I was playing checkers, Mother would set and
listen to the band, as she loves music, classical or no
matter what kind, but anyway she was setting there
one day and between selections the woman next to
her opened up a conversation. She was a woman
about Mother's own age, seventy or seventy-one, and
finally she asked Mother's name and Mother told her
her name and where she was from and Mother asked
her the same question, and who do you think the
woman was?

Well, sir, it was the wife of Frank M. Hartsell, the
man who was engaged to Mother till I stepped in and
cut him out, fifty-two years ago!

Yes, sir!

You can imagine Mother's surprise! And Mrs. Hartsell was surprised, too, when Mother told her she had
once been friends with her husband, tho Mother didn't
say how close friends they had been, or that Mother
and I was the cause of Hartsell going out West. But
that's what he was. Hartsell left his town a month
after the engagement was broke off and ain't never
been back since. He had went out to Michigan and
become a veterinary, and that is where he had settled
down, in Hillsdale, Michigan, and finally married his
wife.

Well, Mother screwed up her courage to ask if
Frank was still living and Mrs. Hartsell took her over
to where they was pitching horse-shoes and there was
old Frank, waiting his turn. And he knowed Mother

as soon as he seen her, tho it was over fifty years. He said he knowed her by her eyes.

"Why, it's Lucy Frost!" he says, and he throwed down his shoes and quit the game.

Then they come over and hunted me up and I will confess I wouldn't of knowed him. Him and I is the same age to the month, but he seems to show it more, some way. He is balder for one thing. And his beard is all white, where mine has still got a streak of brown in it. The very first thing I said to him, I said:

"Well, Frank, that beard of yours makes me feel like I was back north. It looks like a regular blizzard."

"Well," he said, "I guess yourn would be just as white if you had it dry cleaned."

But Mother wouldn't stand that.

"Is that so!" she said to Frank. "Well, Charley ain't had no tobacco in his mouth for over ten years!"

And I ain't!

Well, I excused myself from the checker game and it was pretty close to noon, so we decided to all have dinner together and they was nothing for it only we must try their cafeteria on Third Avenue. It was a little more expensive than ours and not near as good, I thought. I and Mother had about the same dinner we had been having every day and our bill was $1.10. Frank's check was $1.20 for he and his wife. The same meal wouldn't of cost them more than a dollar at our place.

After dinner we made them come up to our house and we all set in the parlor, which the young woman had give us the use of to entertain company. We begun talking over old times and Mother said she was a-scared Mrs. Hartsell would find it tiresome listening to we three talk over old times, but as it turned out they wasn't much chance for nobody else to talk with Mrs. Hartsell in the company. I have heard lots of women that could go it, but Hartsell's wife takes the cake of all the women I ever seen. She told us the family history of everybody in the State of Michigan and bragged for a half hour about her son, who she said is in the drug business in Grand Rapids, and a Rotarian.

When I and Hartsell could get a word in edgeways we joked one another back and forth and I chafed him about being a horse doctor.

"Well, Frank," I said, " you look pretty prosperous, so I suppose they's been plenty of glanders around Hillsdale."

"Well," he said, "I've managed to make more than a fair living. But I've worked pretty hard."

"Yes," I said, "I suppose you get called out all hours of the night to attend births and so on."

Mother made me shut up.

Well, I thought they wouldn't never go home and I and Mother was in misery trying to keep awake, as the both of us generally always take a nap after dinner. Finally they went, after we had made an engagement to meet them in the Park the next morning, and Mrs. Hartsell also invited us to come to their place the next night and play five hundred. But she had forgot that they was a meeting of the Michigan Society that evening, so it was not till two evenings later that we had our first card game.

Hartsell and his wife lived in a house on Third Avenue North and had a private setting room besides their bedroom. Mrs. Hartsell couldn't quit talking about their private setting room like it was something wonderful. We played cards with them, with Mother and Hartsell partners against his wife and I. Mrs. Hartsell is a miserable card player and we certainly got the worst of it.

After the game she brought out a dish of oranges and we had to pretend it was just what we wanted, tho oranges down there is like a young man's whiskers; you enjoy them at first, but they get to be a pesky nuisance.

We played cards again the next night at our place with the same partners and I and Mrs. Hartsell was beat again. Mother and Hartsell was full of compliments for each other on what a good team they made, but the both of them knowed well enough where the secret of their success laid. I guess all and all we must of played ten different evenings and they was only one night when Mrs. Hartsell and I come out ahead. And that one night wasn't no fault of hern.

When we had been down there about two weeks, we spent one evening as their guest in the Congregational Church, at a social give by the Michigan Society. A talk was made by a man named Bitting of Detroit, Michigan, on How I was Cured of Story Telling. He is a big man in the Rotarians and give a witty talk.

A woman named Mrs. Oxford rendered some selections which Mrs. Hartsell said was grand opera music, but whatever they was my daughter Edie could of give her cards and spades and not made such a hullaballoo about it neither.

Then they was a ventriloquist from Grand Rapids and a young woman about forty-five years of age that mimicked different kinds of birds. I whispered to

Mother that they all sounded like a chicken, but she nudged me to shut up.

After the show we stopped in a drug store and I set up the refreshments and it was pretty close to ten o'clock before we finally turned in. Mother and I would of preferred tending the movies, but Mother said we mustn't offend Mrs. Hartsell, tho I asked her had we came to Florida to enjoy ourselves or to just not offend an old chatter-box from Michigan.

I felt sorry for Hartsell one morning. The women folks both had an engagement down to the chiropodist's and I run across Hartsell in the Park and he foolishly offered to play me checkers.

It was him that suggested it, not me, and I guess he repented himself before we had played one game. But he was too stubborn to give up and set there while I beat him game after game and the worst part of it was that a crowd of folks had got in the habit of watching me play and there they all was, looking on, and finally they seen what a fool Frank was making of himself, and they began to chafe him and pass remarks. Like one of them said:

"Who ever told you you was a checker player!"

And

"You might maybe be good for tiddle-de-winks, but not checkers."

I almost felt like letting him beat me a couple games. But the crowd would of knowed it was a put up job.

Well, the women folks joined us in the Park and I wasn't going to mention our little game, but Hartsell told about it himself and admitted he wasn't no match for me.

"Well," said Mrs. Hartsell, "checkers ain't much of

a game anyway, is it?" She said: "It's more of a children's game, ain't it? At least, I know my boy's children used to play it a good deal."

"Yes, ma'am," I said. "It's a children's game the way your husband plays it, too."

Mother wanted to smooth things over, so she said:

"Maybe they's other games where Frank can beat you."

"Yes," said Mrs. Hartsell, "and I bet he could beat you pitching horseshoes."

"Well," I said, "I would give him a chance to try, only I ain't pitched a shoe in over sixteen years."

"Well," said Hartsell, "I ain't played checkers in twenty years."

"You ain't never played it," I said.

"Anyway," says Frank, "Lucy and I is your master at five hundred."

Well, I could of told him why that was, but had decency enough to hold my tongue.

It had got so now that he wanted to play cards every night and when I or Mother wanted to go to a movie, any one of us would have to pretend we had a headache and then trust to goodness that they wouldn't see us sneak into the theater. I don't mind playing cards when my partner keeps their mind on the game, but you take a woman like Hartsell's wife and how can they play cards when they have got to stop every couple seconds and brag about their son in Grand Rapids?

Well, the New York-New Jersey Society announced that they was goin' to give a social evening too, and I said to Mother, I said:

"Well, that is one evening when we will have an excuse not to play five hundred."

"Yes," she said, "but we will have to ask Frank and his wife to go to the social with us as they asked us to go to the Michigan social."

"Well," I said, "I had rather stay home than drag that chatterbox everywheres we go."

So Mother said:

"You are getting too cranky. Maybe she does talk a little too much but she is good hearted. And Frank is always good company."

So I said:

"I suppose if he is such good company you wished you had of married him."

Mother laughed and said I sounded like I was jealous. Jealous of a cow doctor!

Anyway we had to drag them along to the social and I will say that we give them a much better entertainment than they had given us.

Judge Lane of Paterson made a fine talk on business conditions and a Mrs. Newell of Westfield imitated birds, only you could really tell what they was the way she done it. Two young women from Red Bank sung a choral selection and we clapped them back and they gave us Home to Our Mountains and Mother and Mrs. Hartsell both had tears in their eyes. And Hartsell, too.

Well, some way or another the chairman got wind that I was there and asked me to make a talk and I wasn't even going to get up, but Mother made me, so I got up and said:

"Ladies and gentlemen," I said. "I didn't expect to be called on for a speech on an occasion like this or no other occasion as I do not set myself up as a speech maker, so will have to do the best I can, which I often say is the best anybody can do."

Then I told them the story about Pat and the motor-cycle, using the brogue, and it seemed to tickle them and I told them one or two other stories, but altogether I wasn't on my feet more than twenty or twenty-five minutes and you ought to of heard the clapping and hollering when I set down.   Even Mrs. Hartsell admitted that I am quite a speechifier and said if I ever went to Grand Rapids, Michigan, her son would make me talk to the Rotarians.

When it was over, Hartsell wanted we should go to their house and play cards, but his wife reminded him that it was after 9:30 P. M., rather a late hour to start a card game, but he had went crazy on the sub-ject of cards, probably because he didn't have to play partners with his wife.   Anyway, we got rid of them and went home to bed.

It was the next morning, when we met over to the Park, that Mrs. Hartsell made the remark that she wasn't getting no exercise, so I suggested that why didn't she take part in the roque game.

She said she had not played a game of roque in twenty years, but if Mother would play she would play.   Well, at first Mother wouldn't hear of it, but finally consented, more to please Mrs. Hartsell than anything else.

Well, they had a game with a Mrs. Ryan from Eagle, Nebraska, and a young Mrs. Morse from Rutland, Vermont, who Mother had met down to the chiropo-dist's.   Well, Mother couldn't hit a flea and they all laughed at her and I couldn't help from laughing at her myself and finally she quit and said her back was too lame to stoop over.   So they got another lady and kept on playing and soon Mrs. Hartsell was the one everybody was laughing at, as she had a long shot to hit the black ball, and as she made the effort her teeth fell out on to the court. I never seen a woman so flustered in my life. And I never heard so much laughing, only Mrs. Hartsell didn't join in and she was madder than a hornet and wouldn't play no more, so the game broke up.

Mrs. Hartsell went home without speaking to nobody, but Hartsell stayed around and finally he said to me, he said:

"Well, I played you checkers the other day and you beat me bad and now what do you say if you and me play a game of horseshoes?"

I told him I hadn't pitched a shoe in sixteen years, but Mother said:

"Go ahead and play. You used to be good at it and maybe it will come back to you."

Well, to make a long story short, I give in. I oughtn't to of never tried it, as I hadn't pitched a shoe in sixteen years, and I only done it to humor Hartsell.

Before we started, Mother patted me on the back and told me to do my best, so we started in and I seen right off that I was in for it, as I hadn't pitched a shoe in sixteen years and didn't have my distance. And besides, the plating had wore off the shoes so that they was points right where they stuck into my thumb and I hadn't throwed more than two or three times when my thumb was raw and it pretty near killed me to hang on to the shoe, let alone pitch it.

Well, Hartsell throws the awkwardest shoe I ever seen pitched and to see him pitch you wouldn't think he would ever come nowheres near, but he is also the luckiest pitcher I ever seen and he made some pitches where the shoe lit five and six feet short and then

schoonered up and was a ringer. They's no use trying
to beat that kind of luck.

They was a pretty fair size crowd watching us and
four or five other ladies besides Mother, and it seems
like, when Hartsell pitches, he has got to chew and it
kept the ladies on the anxious seat as he don't seem
to care which way he is facing when he leaves go.

You would think a man as old as him would of
learnt more manners.

Well, to make a long story short, I was just beginning to get my distance when I had to give up on
account of my thumb, which I showed it to Hartsell
and he seen I couldn't go on, as it was raw and bleeding. Even if I could of stood it to go on myself,
Mother wouldn't of allowed it after she seen my
thumb. So anyway I quit and Hartsell said the score
was nineteen to six, but I don't know what it was.
Or don't care, neither.

Well, Mother and I went home and I said I hoped
we was through with the Hartsells as I was sick and
tired of them, but it seemed like she had promised
we would go over to their house that evening for
another game of their everlasting cards.

Well, my thumb was giving me considerable pain
and I felt kind of out of sorts and I guess maybe I
forgot myself, but anyway, when we was about through
playing Hartsell made the remark that he wouldn't
never lose a game of cards if he could always have
Mother for a partner.

So I said:

"Well, you had a chance fifty years ago to always
have her for a partner, but you wasn't man enough to
keep her."

I was sorry the minute I had said it and Hartsell

didn't know what to say and for once his wife couldn't say nothing. Mother tried to smooth things over by making the remark that I must of had something stronger than tea or I wouldn't talk so silly. But Mrs. Hartsell had froze up like an iceberg and hardly said good night to us and I bet her and Frank put in a pleasant hour after we was gone.

As we was leaving, Mother said to him: "Never mind Charley's nonsense, Frank. He is just mad because you beat him all hollow pitching horseshoes and playing cards."

She said that to make up for my slip, but at the same time she certainly riled me. I tried to keep ahold of myself, but as soon as we was out of the house she had to open up the subject and begun to scold me for the break I had made.

Well, I wasn't in no mood to be scolded. So I said: "I guess he is such a wonderful pitcher and card player that you wished you had married him."

"Well," she said, "at least he ain't a baby to give up pitching because his thumb has got a few scratches."

"And how about you," I said, "making a fool of yourself on the roque court and then pretending your back is lame and you can't play no more!"

"Yes," she said, "but when you hurt your thumb I didn't laugh at you, and why did you laugh at me when I sprained my back?"

"Who could help from laughing!" I said.

"Well," she said, "Frank Hartsell didn't laugh."

"Well," I said, "why didn't you marry him?"

"Well," said Mother, "I almost wished I had!"

"And I wished so, too!" I said.

"I'll remember that!" said Mother, and that's the last word she said to me for two days.

We seen the Hartsells the next day in the Park and I was willing to apologize, but they just nodded to us. And a couple days later we heard they had left for Orlando, where they have got relatives.

I wished they had went there in the first place.

Mother and I made it up setting on a bench.

"Listen, Charley," she said. "This is our Golden Honeymoon and we don't want the whole thing spoilt with a silly old quarrel."

"Well," I said, "did you mean that about wishing you had married Hartsell?"

"Of course not," she said, "that is, if you didn't mean that you wished I had, too."

So I said:

"I was just tired and all wrought up. I thank God you chose me instead of him as they's no other woman in the world who I could of lived with all these years."

"How about Mrs. Hartsell?" says Mother.

"Good gracious!" I said. "Imagine being married to a woman that plays five hundred like she does and drops her teeth on the roque court!"

"Well," said Mother, "it wouldn't be no worse than being married to a man that expectorates towards ladies and is such a fool in a checker game."

So I put my arm around her shoulder and she stroked my hand and I guess we got kind of spoony.

They was two days left of our stay in St. Petersburg and the next to the last day Mother introduced me to a Mrs. Kendall from Kingston, Rhode Island, who she had met at the chiropodist's.

Mrs. Kendall made us acquainted with her husband, who is in the grocery business. They have got two sons and five grandchildren and one great-grandchild.

One of their sons lives in Providence and is way up in the Elks as well as a Rotarian.

We found them very congenial people and we played cards with them the last two nights we was there. They was both experts and I only wished we had met them sooner instead of running into the Hartsells. But the Kendalls will all be there again next winter and we will see more of them, that is, if we decide to make the trip again.

We left the Sunshine City on the eleventh day of February, at 11 A. M. This give us a day trip through Florida and we seen all the country we had passed through at night on the way down.

We reached Jacksonville at 7 P. M. and pulled out of there at 8:30 P. M. We reached Fayetteville, North Carolina, at nine o'clock the following morning, and reached Washington, D. C., at 6:30 P. M., laying over there half an hour.

We reached Trenton at 11:01 P. M. and had wired ahead to my daughter and son-in-law and they met us at the train and we went to their house and they put us up for the night. John would of made us stay up all night, telling about our trip, but Edie said we must be tired and made us go to bed. That's my daughter.

The next day we took our train for home and arrived safe and sound, having been gone just one month and a day.

Here comes Mother, so I guess I better shut up.